Pig In A Poke
J. Arens

Big Town Publishing

Copyright © 2025 by J. Arens

Cover Art by Salient Books

www.salientbooks.shop

Edited by: E. Paige Spear

CollaborativePassages.org

First edition 2025

ISBN: 979-8-9878005-8-4 (Softcover)

ISBN: 979-8-9893041-1-0 (Ebook)

Published by: Big Town Publishing

districtdetectives.com

Contents

**To Those Special Few
That always seem to fall into
good fortune**

Chapter 1
The One With The Change of Plans

Razor smiled at her and he walked over to the cabinet and leaned on the top edge of it loosely. "Get home safe, Olli." He smiled at her softly. "And maybe next time, if Monte's under the weather, and a storm's blowing in off the water...stay at the office or go home? I worry about you."

Olli stood up as far as the ceiling of the tunnel would allow her and looked at him for a moment. She tilted her head. "Always. I can take care of myself. I've gotten in and out of The District a couple of times without Monte."

Razor nodded and smirked at the tone she used. "Good girl. Tell him get well for me? Maybe bring him some soup. <u>After</u> you go home and get some sleep." He smirked at her and winked. "Thanks for stopping by, Doll." He pushed the cabinet closed firmly.

Olli stood in the dark for a couple of seconds and shook her head. Just when she had almost managed to convince herself—Dallas too—that there wasn't anything strange going on between her and Razor...

Things like this tended to happen.

And he said things like that.

Olli huffed a little and reached out into the darkness with a practiced movement. A small click and a string of dim lights blinked on. "Oh. He fixed that light." She made an amused noise when she looked at the fourth bulb down on the string. "How very thoughtful of him," she muttered to herself. She shrugged to herself and walked down the hallway quickly, moving with the ease of many years of practice.

She couldn't even remember how many times she walked down this particular tunnel.

There were <u>many</u> tunnels in The District. But it seemed this one was one of her most traveled.

Olli frowned a little to herself as she walked.

She got tripped up in Razor's headquarters too many times. Anthony—Razor—DeLuca wasn't dangerous in the sense that he would kill her on sight, he was much more clever than that. Which is where the danger came in. Despite the fact that he often made Olli's life hard and convoluted, he was also the only mob boss she could interact with without worry of being shot.

Plus, she loved matching wits with him.

Part of the cleverness came from his constant ability to set up traps and tricks to keep his headquarters from being invaded.

The obstacle course to get from one of the many entrances to the office in the center of the large building was brutal. And nearly always changing.

It was certainly one of the most interesting places in The District.

The District.

A sprawling section of town made up of warehouses and tenement buildings. All of them built just before and during The Great War. Hastily thrown together to house the workers for the docks and war building efforts. The Harbor had made Big Town the perfect place for submarines, destroyers, and troop carriers to be built.

Along with a healthy dose of munitions.

With the war effort came the money. And with the money came the bigger houses and businesses on the edge of town. By the time the Roaring Twenties swept through Big Town, the entire town had shifted to the East, leaving behind The Harbor, the warehouses and the tenement buildings. Abandoning the haunting reminders of the war and following the siren song of good times and affluence.

But not <u>all</u> of Big Town's residents left The District. Joey Leftfoot stayed. Big Town's first mafia don. He and the men in his crime family saw the opportunity swirling in the abandoned part of Big Town and took it upon themselves to snap it up.

The District became so dangerous—between the buildings and the men—that no one dared to cross The Line.

No one except The District Detective.

Alan Wainwright had held the title for most of Olli's life. And when her grandfather had retired, handing over the reins of WDA to his son, Olli realized her dream and stepped into The District Detective Office.

A half-dozen turns down three ladders and two flights of stairs. Olli was deep underground, below the building where Razor kept his headquarters.

Olli paused at a corner where three tunnels intersected. She reached into her inner pocket of her black leather jacket and pulled out a round mirror that was about the size of her palm. She wasn't sure, but she thought that she heard something. This was a much better option than simply sticking her head around the corner.

Getting caught for the <u>second</u> time in less than twenty-four hours...well, that hadn't happened to her in a long time. And she wasn't about to let that happen to her today.

Olli had already spent a few hours too many upstairs, and she was ready to get back to the comfort of her office and maybe her own bed. She shifted her weight a little more to the corner and picked the mirror up to eye-level while tilting it out so she could see around the corner.

After a couple of seconds of tilting the mirror this way and that way, Olli was satisfied that the hallway was empty.

Apparently, the noise that she heard was all in her head.

Good. She needed to get out of here.

Home was calling her name. She also wanted to check on Monte. He never got sick. Razor was right. He could probably use some soup.

Olli walked down the hallway to her right and slightly forward.

It was the closest to an exit.

Three hallways later, Olli was finally in the homestretch. She walked toward the end of the last tunnel, a smile starting to build on her face. A couple more feet, a ladder, and a small hatch was all that stood between her and the outside world of The District.

When she was about two-thirds of the way down the hall, the cold hit her. Olli walked a little further and rubbed her hands together a bit. She looked at the metal escape ladder two paces in front of her and ran the zipper of her leather jacket as far as it would go.

"Looks frosty," she mused to herself as she flipped her collar up close to her neck. It had dropped a handful of degrees just walking up to the ladder. Olli walked up to the ladder and grabbed the first rung, one above her head. "<u>Aces!</u>" She pulled her hand back and pulled her sleeves over her hands as far as they would go. She started to climb quickly, muttering under her breath about how cold the metal was.

But her problems only got worse.

Olli slammed into the hatch at the top of the half frozen ladder and pursed her lips when it creaked a little but didn't move. She looked at her shoulder and pulled a face at the frost on the black leather of her jacket. "Aces...that's bad." She climbed up one more rung and pushed her shoulder up against the hatch.

This time it didn't even creak.

Olli stood where she was for a moment, bent over up against the hatch, standing one too many rungs up. She shook her head and closed her eyes. "Aces."

Never one to be outdone by a frozen door, Olli hurried down the ladder. About two-thirds of the way down, she gave up. Olli jumped down the rest of the way and yanked her hands out of her sleeves. She rubbed them together and cupped them over her mouth and blew on them.

She went down the tunnel and doubled back across to a third tunnel. A few more tunnels and she walked up to a boring-looking door.

Olli turned the knob while she walked, ready for the door to swing open.

It didn't.

Instead, Olli crashed into the door with all her weight.

Olli took half a step back and looked at the door like it was a completely foreign object. She rubbed her shoulder and pulled a confused face. "Aces!"

A quick glanced over the door and it was obvious it wasn't going to be swinging anytime soon. There was a heavy frost on the hinges that saw to that.

Olli stood where she was for a moment and jiggled the knob a little. "Well...if it was <u>that</u> simple, everyone would be doing it..." She thought for a moment and turned around. There was one more place she would be able to get out.

Olli stood at the end of a hallway almost halfway across the building and looked at the mess in front of her. She couldn't believe her terrible luck.

How did things like this happen to good people?

Piled in front of her in a jumble was a large tangle of what looked like broken chairs and a few tables.

"What...what _is_ this?!" Olli gestured around at the mess in frustration. She pivoted and looked back at the tunnel she was standing in. There were more ways out, but none of them that she could get to where she was.

What was she supposed to do now?"

Olli tilted her chin down into her jacket collar. "Dee? Can you hear me?" she wondered, hoping that the small mic sewn into the shirt would work. If she could get through to her, then maybe a plan could be made to get Olli out.

Static hissed back at her like an angry snake for a couple of seconds before turning off.

Olli nodded a little in a slow way and grunted to herself. "Aces ...Of course not."

She stood where she was for much longer than she should have, debating over which plan would get her out of the jam she was in fastest. Olli blinked and shook herself a little after almost ten minutes of staring off into the distance.

Standing here, staring at the half-dark around her wasn't going to help her.

At all.

There was one more way out of the building. It wasn't the best option. In fact, it was more like the absolute _worst_ option.

Olli sighed and started forward, her pace brisk and with sharp purpose.

Going upstairs, trying to avoid being caught again, and walking out the front door was going to be nigh on impossible, but she was going to try it.

Nothing wagered, nothing gained.

Go big or go home...

Except that in this case, it was more like '—go big or get locked up somewhere in the basement of Razor's headquarters. Again—'.

Olli started up a narrow, tightly twisted spiral staircase and mentally prepared herself for the next part of her adventure.

There were going to be so many goons between her and the outside world. This was going to be tricky.

Olli walked into a matching narrow hall. She walked along at a brisk pace, her shoulders stooped over to miss the ceiling.

Olli pulled her lips back a little and very carefully clicked the door in front of her shut. The slight click made her wince and hold her breath. She closed her eyes tightly for a moment before slowly opening one and leaning slightly to see out of the crack created.

On the other side of the door was a piece of wall that made up a section of hallway in the main part of Razor's headquarters. Which were, apparently, extremely busy.

Olli thought for a moment and shrugged to herself. She could wait a few minutes and see if the halls got a little more empty.

She had cracked the door open almost twenty minutes before. Not far, barely enough that she could see through the crack, if she leaned her head back and forth. The small shaft of light had nearly blinded her after spending so much time in the dark tunnels. And it did absolutely no good. She had never seen so many people in Razor's headquarters.

Apparently, the snowstorm that had grounded her had driven in the minions as well. There wasn't a single break in foot traffic. It was like standing on the edge of the biggest thoroughfare that ran through Eminences. They were using the time to catch up together. No one seemed to notice the one wall joint opened a few inches.

Olli leaned her forehead against the wall in front of her for a moment and closed her eyes. She sighed a little, picked her head up, and shook her head. "Aces," she grumbled to herself.

It was official. There was no way out. At least, not at the moment. She had already been standing there too long.

Olli took a heavy breath and gently pushed the door in the wall closed. It clicked softly and completely sealed off the hallway again. She blew a small breath out between her lips and put her hands on her hips. What was she going to do now?

The soft click off to his right broke his concentration.

The glass froze almost to his lips.

He carefully set the glass down on the desk in front of him. While he looked in the direction the click came from; he carefully slipped a small drawer open that was at the top edge of the desk, perfectly molded into the decorative edge.

He pulled the small derringer out of the shallow drawer.

Razor pivoted to face the cabinet with the derringer pointed in front of him, cocking it at the same time. He blinked. "Olli?!"

Olli stepped out of the tunnel and froze when she saw him. "What are you doing?" She stood up and out of the cabinet and pushed the door closed.

"I was going to ask you the same thing," Razor mused, tilting his head. "You _left_."

Olli shrugged and finished stepping completely into the office. She closed the cabinet and half pointed at him. "Mind pointing that pea-shooter in any other direction?"

Razor blinked and seemed to snap out of the shock. "Oh gracious. Right. Terribly sorry." He pivoted and gently set the derringer back in its hiding spot.

Olli tilted an eyebrow and watched him like she wasn't sure who he was anymore. "Two questions?"

"And those would be?" Razor looked at her, leaning his arm on the desk casually.

"You were going to shoot me?"

"Well, in my defense...I didn't _know_ it was you."

"Which leads me to my next question..." Olli shifted and tilted her head. "You have a _gun_?"

Razor closed the shallow drawer into his desk and smirked. "It's a derringer," he downplayed.

Olli invited herself back into the chair she had been sitting in after unzipping her jacket. She draped her arms over the armrests of the chair and tilted her head.

"Yes..." Razor shrugged and reached for the glass on his desk like nothing had happened. He took a small drink and grunted. "Can never be too careful."

Olli stood where she was for a minute, still trying to process the information. "Careful," she repeated. "I'm inclined to agree. I just didn't realize that you had one <u>on</u> you." She looked around the office and then back to him. "And it seems to me you're pretty safe on that side of the desk..."

"A lot of people have guns, Doll." Razor shrugged and tilted his head. He swirled his drink and shook his head. "And I'm not sure that I'm as safe here on this side of the desk as you say I am."

"Well, yeah. Sure. But you're <u>hardly</u> 'lots of people'." Olli's eyebrows went up.

"You seem...disappointed?" Razor wondered, one eyebrow going up slightly.

Olli took a breath and hummed a little. "Yeah. That sounds close to what I'm feeling.

"About me having a gun? I don't understand."

"It just seems so...<u>pedestrian</u> of you. I guess I expect more from the guy that can rig up half a hallway floor to spin like a carousel." Olli smirked.

Razor smirked at her. "Why are you here?" He chuckled softly and sipped his drink. "I thought you had left to go home."

"You've finally done it." Olli shrugged. She leaned back into her chair a bit more and adjusted her jacket around her ribs a bit.

Razor looked at her for a moment and tilted his head. "Done what?"

"You've finally got a headquarters that I can't escape from." Olli gestured around vaguely. "I don't know if I should congratulate you, or be irritated that I couldn't out-think this problem."

Razor looked at her and smirked. "And you came back <u>here</u>?" He pointed down at the floor of the office slightly and tilted his head. "What on earth for?"

"Had to tell you the good news myself." Olli shrugged. "Figured you'd be proud of yourself. You've been trying for <u>years</u> to make this place escape proof."

Razor shook his head a little and waved his hand a little. "Actually...that's...no-no." He half-laughed and shook his head again. "That's not what all that the traps and tricks are for."

Olli blinked a couple of times and tilted her head. "I don't...understand."

"I put those in place to make sure no one can get <u>in</u>." Razor pointed in the general direction of the rest of the building.

"But I get in all the time?" Olli protested.

"And that's because you are <u>very</u> special." Razor smirked at her. "You also end up here quite a bit."

Olli snorted. "Pretty elaborate way to lock yourself away from the rest of the world."

"Or. A clever way to make sure that I have a few minutes to escape, should anyone want to kill me."

"What about arresting you?"

Razor chuckled. "You make me laugh." He took a sip of his drink and looked at Olli with her eyebrows up slightly. "Why <u>are</u> you back in my office instead of braving the elements?"

"Everything's iced over. Couldn't break out. And that weather that you were just talking about? Drove all your boys here. <u>And</u> since they don't know I'm here, I thought it wise to keep from being noticed. It's cold down in the tunnels. And I figured you wouldn't mind telling me another story. Or the company." Olli shrugged and half shook her head.

Razor nodded. "That makes sense. So. Another story?"

Olli shrugged and bobbed her head. "Just to pass the time..."

A smile brightened Razor's face. "Wonderful!"

Chapter 2
The One With The Pig-In-A-Poke

Olli shrugged. "Why not, right?" She smirked a bit and leaned back heavily into the chair. "I've got nothing else to do until the storm lets up, or you tell me about a different way out of here where <u>they</u> won't notice me."

"What makes you think that I have a way out of here where the men who work for me wouldn't see you?"

Olli looked at him blandly. Her chin dropped toward her left shoulder slightly. "Razor."

"Yes?"

"This is <u>you</u> we're talking about here. Which means you do. Don't you always have an exit plan?"

Razor nodded and shrugged slightly. "What makes you think that I would share it with <u>you</u>?"

Olli shrugged. "Why not? You do me favors all the time."

"That's a bit more than just a favor." Razor shook his head. "What if I need to escape because <u>you're</u> the one looking for me?"

Olli laughed a little and shook her head. "Got another story to tell me?"

Razor nodded. "Sure." He set down his empty glass and adjusted in his chair. "Sure. Anything in particular?"

Olli shook her head. "No. Whatever you want, really."

Razor nodded slowly. He pursed his lips a bit and stared off into the middle distance for a moment before looking at her. "Another con?"

Olli bobbed her head. "Sure. Sounds good to me." She adjusted how she was sitting and folded her right leg up and under her left. She rested her left arm across her ribs and her right elbow on the arm of the chair.

Razor reached over her and unlocked a humidor box. He fished out a cigar and snipped the end. Once he had it lit, he leaned back in his chair and puffed on the cigar for a moment. "Let's see..." He blew the bluish-grey smoke toward the ceiling quietly.

Olli watched him and glanced at the smoke as it floated up. She glanced at him and cleared her throat a little. "Razor?"

Razor made a small noise in the back of his throat and looked at her. "Sorry, Doll." He cleared his throat. "I have a question for you."

Olli nodded and made a humming noise in her throat. "What's that?"

"Pig-In-A-Poke." Razor looked at her like he was gauging her reaction.

Olli sat for a moment, seemingly waiting for him to go on before she cleared her throat. "Is there a question in there some-where?" she wondered.

"Do you know it?"

Olli bit her lip and looked thoughtful for a moment. "It sounds familiar..."

"Take a stab."

"It has something to do with a pig?" Olli offered, her tone heavily skeptical.

Razor chuckled and nodded. "Historically. Yes."

"All right. Tell me about how a pig has anything to do with this con." Olli leaned forward, resting her elbows on her knees. "Paint me the picture of how the con works so I can be overly impressed at how you managed to twist it into your own crazy con."

"Crazy con?!" Razor protested, looking insulted.

Olli scoffed and smirked. "Aces. Don't be like that!"

Razor clicked his tongue a couple of times. "All right." He puffed on his cigar for a second and looked at her shrewdly. "So. Pig-In-A-Poke is probably the oldest known con there is."

Olli grunted a little. "Does that mean that you've known it your whole life then?"

Razor looked at her. "My father first told me about it when I was a young boy, yes. But I wouldn't say my _whole_ life."

Olli laughed. "You're talking like it's the greatest of all cons. The Holy Grail of grifters."

Razor puffed on his cigar and tilted his head a little. He slowly pulled the cigar out of his mouth. "You know...It almost is."

Olli blinked. "Aces...really?" She looked at him closely and one eyebrow went up slowly. "Must be a _really_ impressive con."

"Any con man worth his salt knows it. And have done it. It's so simply elegant that it seems...easy. But really, just between you and me, like all great things that <u>seem</u> easy...it's actually one of the hardest cons to pull off."

Olli raised her eyebrows a little and leaned back in her chair. "You don't say."

"I know you're mocking me, Olli. You really shouldn't."

Olli snorted. She smirked a little and held up a hand. "All right. You're right. I'm sorry. I'm just a little cranky. Being locked in a place like this when you're someone like me tends to make that happen." She shifted a little and stopped smirking. "What makes it so hard?"

"There's no...frills. No props. Nothing to...hide behind." Razor gestured a little with his cigar hand. "It comes down to the complete and total ability of the person to convince whomever that things are the way that they say they are."

Olli nodded. "How many players?"

Razor tilted his head and puffed on his cigar. "As little as two."

"Con man and mark?" Olli assumed, one eyebrow going up slightly. She leaned forward and started shifting around awkwardly while she shook her arms out of her leather jacket. After a minute of flailing around, Olli finally managed to get herself out of the clutches of the jacket.

Razor quietly watched her work her way out of the jacket before he smiled and nodded. "Clever girl."

Olli shrugged a little and hummed. "Color me officially intrigued."

Razor looked at her for a moment and shook his head. "All right. So. What do you know about the con?"

Olli looked thoughtful for a minute. "It's so simple, it's deceptively hard to pull off well." She held up her first finger. "It's the oldest con that you know about," another finger went up, "And it's a popular con..."

"Do you know how it started?"

Olli shrugged. "Why don't you tell me."

"Killing time?"

Olli shrugged and gestured around herself. "Like I have anywhere better to be?"

Razor's left eyebrow went up fractionally for a split second before he leaned back into his chair. "It dates back to the middle ages—" he puffed on his cigar. "Back when meat was especially scarce. Someone would put a cat in a bag, and then try to pass it off as a piglet."

Olli nodded and grunted slightly. "Did it work?"

"Sometimes, yes. Other times no." Razor shrugged and smirked slightly.

"Did you ever try to?" Olli wondered, looking at him hopefully.

"No, I didn't try to pass a cat as a pig."

Olli pouted a little. "Aw. Aces...why not?"

"Because that's the very basic principle of the con. After that is grasped, you can build it into whatever you want it to be."

Olli nodded and looked at him for a minute. "All right. Sounds a little bit like an excuse to me...What's the craziest thing you've ever ran this con for?"

Razor puffed on the cigar for a moment and made a thoughtful noise. He blew the smoke up toward the ceiling and watched it.

Olli watched him and tilted her head. She waited a little longer before she tipped her head a little. "Really. I would have thought that you would have had a wild story to attach to that." She frowned a little and shook her head slightly. "I'm almost disappo inted..."

Razor looked at her through the cigar smoke and smirked. "Sorry to keep you waiting, Doll. I had to choose one."

Olli looked at him closely for a moment before she slowly smirked. "More than one? I like the sounds of that."

Razor put his cigar between his teeth and held his hands out to the side a little. He turned his fingers toward himself and then back out again. His left hand reached up and pulled the cigar out of his mouth. "Really, Doll...It is me."

Olli scoffed. "Aces. All right." She looked at him closely. "Which is the best one? I want to hear about that."

Razor smirked. "It's a toss-up."

"Between?" Olli pried.

"The Tower of Pisa, and the Liberty Bell."

Olli stared at him for a moment before she started to laugh. She laughed more and rubbed her face. A small humming noise escaped her as she sighed. "Ohhhhhhhhhhhh, you really had me going there for a second."

"What is that supposed to mean?" Insult crossed Razor's face. "You think I'm lying?"

"I think you're a con man that's telling me stories." Olli looked at him and raised her eyebrows a little. "I'd say we're getting dangerously close to that territory."

Razor clicked his tongue sharply. "Have I ever lied to you?"

"To my face directly?" Olli tilted her head. "Not blatantly...but we both know that you have lied by omission many times."

Razor looked insulted for a split second before he nodded slowly. "You caught that, hm?"

"I learned from the best." Olli shrugged and bobbed her head. "I was told that I can always count on you doing whatever is best for <u>you</u>."

Razor shrugged a little and nodded. "He's not wrong."

Olli smirked and looked at him. "The <u>Leaning Tower of Pisa</u>." She raised an eyebrow.

Razor nodded. "And the Liberty Bell."

"When were you in Philly?! I thought you came straight here from Italy?"

Razor smirked. "Who said that I was in Philly?"

Olli blinked and pulled her head back. "You weren't."

Razor shook his head. "I was not. I find it's much easier to pull this con off with something famous if you're not close enough to actually go and see it."

Olli looked at him in a thoughtful way for a moment before she grunted and nodded. "I guess that makes sense. Where were you?"

"Italy."

"When you sold the tower of Pisa?" Olli tilted her head.

Razor shook his head. "Heavens, no." He smirked. "When I sold the Liberty Bell."

Olli stared at him for a moment. She blinked sharply a couple of times and she snorted. "<u>Aces</u>!"

Razor smirked. "You'll notice that my American accent is quite convincing here...over there, it's even better."

Olli narrowed her eyes. "You learned English for the strict reason of trying to pawn off the Liberty Bell...in Italy."

Razor shrugged. "Not for that reason <u>alone</u>...it just came up as an opportunity, and I wasn't about to miss the chance."

Olli scoffed and shook her head. "All right then...tell me how this...<u>opportunity</u> came up?"

"You want me to tell you about the Liberty Bell. Not Pisa?"

Olli looked thoughtful for a minute before she shrugged. "Liberty Bell first. And then maybe...maybe we'll talk about Pisa."

"Did I ever tell you how I met Joey?"

"You went looking for him?"

Razor shook his head. "I tried to sell him Pisa."

Olli stared at him. "What."

Razor smirked. "So...thoughts on which story you'd like to hear?"

Olli sat where she was for a moment, not moving. "That's...a hard choice."

Razor leaned back in his chair and put his cigar between his lips. He puffed a little and waited patiently.

Chapter 3
The One With The Arrival

Olli looked at him for a moment longer before she cleared her throat. "This is a really hard choice."

Razor chuckled quietly and puffed on his cigar. "Come on, Doll. Time's wasting."

Olli nodded. "Right. You tried to sell Joey Leftfoot the Leaning Tower of Pisa?" She looked at him with as much skepticism as was in her tone.

Razor shrugged. "Why not?"

"And you got a job out of it?"

"Again...why not?"

Olli looked at him with some confusion. "All right. Tell me why he would."

"Because I'm clever."

Olli snorted. "Right...I want to hear about that one."

Razor nodded a little and shifted in his chair. "I think I can handle that."

Olli made a thoughtful noise. "I have one more question before you get started."

Razor grunted a little and looked at her expectantly. "And that would be?"

"Did you talk like this? Or were you using an Italian accent?"

Razor laughed and shook his head. "That's what's important for you to know?"

Olli shrugged. "You said you talked like an American over there trying to sell the Liberty Bell..."

"Well, yeah, that was there. Couldn't sound like I was from there. They would have never believed me and my story if I didn't sound like I was American!" Razor chuckled and smirked at her.

Olli scoff-giggled a little and nodded. "That's a fair point." She looked at him shrewdly. "All right. Tell me about how you conned Joey Leftfoot." She smirked. "And somehow didn't <u>disappear</u>."

"Technically, I didn't...<u>actually</u> con him."

"No, because then you'd be dead," Olli pointed out in a dry tone, a small smirk on her face.

Razor grunted slightly and bobbed his head. "There's a very good possibility of that."

Olli wrinkled her nose and nodded.

"Course, there's a very good chance you would be, too."

Olli pursed her lips and frowned a little. "Right." She folded her arms across her ribs loosely and bobbed her head. "Aces. On <u>that</u> note...tell me why you chose Joey."

Razor smirked and puffed on his cigar thoughtfully. "It's been almost...twenty years since I got off the boat. I was still Anthony then..."

Anthony looked up when the boat horn sounded off.

They would be docking soon.

He couldn't believe it. It didn't even feel real.

He had waited so long for this moment.

America at last.

"New York?" Olli wondered.

"Well. That <u>has</u> to be some sort of record," Razor mused dryly. "What was that? Fifteen seconds?"

Olli held her arms out. "It's important to the story!"

"Why is it important?" Razor tilted his head.

"Because details matter." Olli smirked. "Did you take a train down from New York? A plane—"

"You think I had money to <u>fly</u> here from New York?!" Razor scoffed, his eyebrows jumping up wildly. He chuckled. "How could I have possibly afforded that?"

Olli shrugged. "Con money."

"You mean the money I spent on the ticket to get on the boat?" Razor mused skeptically.

"You didn't con your way onto the ship?!" Olli laughed. "I...I don't know if I'm impressed...or a little disappointed."

Razor snorted and shook his head a little. "I may not have conned my way onto the ship, but there's a good chance that the way there had a half dozen cons."

Olli smirked a little and snorted. "You don't say."

Razor shrugged a little and bobbed his head. "Fella's gotta eat."

"And make some extra spending cash," Olli assumed, tilting her head slightly.

Razor shrugged a little and smirked. "Trips halfway across the world can be expensive. And it's a long ride over the ocean."

Olli nodded and smirked. "<u>That</u> makes sense."

Anthony glanced around, watching as the people on the deck around him started to pick themselves up and walk to the bow of the boat.

They were just as excited to see land as he was. It had been almost a full five days since they had left Italy.

It had been nothing but waves around and the sky above them since then.

The trip had been smooth. No storms had interrupted their journey, and the ocean had been relatively smooth.

Anthony stood up from his lounge chair and closed his book gently.

"There it is," Olli mused dryly.

Razor looked at her and tilted his head slightly. "Hm?"

"How in the world did you manage a first-class ticket on an ocean liner?" Olli looked at him and smirked.

"I wasn't first class."

"Would that be <u>before</u> you bought your ticket? Or was that when you walked <u>onto</u> the ship?" Olli looked at him shrewdly.

Razor sat where he was for a moment and stared back at her. He shrugged slightly. "All right. I was <u>second</u> class, if that will smooth your feathers."

"A lounge chair, a book, <u>and</u> second class. Fancy."

Razor tipped an eyebrow. "I think it was the most relaxing five days at sea I've ever had."

Olli smirked a little and shook her head. "Sounds like a nice vacation."

"It <u>really</u> was. You should try it sometime."

"What's that?" Olli tilted her head. "A vacation?"

"Something to consider." Razor smirked. "So. I packed my things up..."

Once he tucked the book under his arm, Anthony walked after the rest of the people on the deck. He wanted to see land just as eagerly as the rest of them.

The water was exciting at first, but now that it had been almost a full week on the ocean, standing on solid ground appealed to everyone on the ship.

Anthony stopped two people back from the railing and looked past their heads to see what was in front of them.

It was a large harbor, and looked a little like the harbor they had left back in Italy with boats coming in and out. the bustle of the traffic heading out to sea, or coming into port the same time as they were. A large barge was floating into port, pushed along with two hard-working tugboats.

Most of the seafaring vessels weren't carrying people. It looked like most were industrial in nature.

As he stood surveying the scene in front of him, he realized that most of the ships containing the industrial materials were heading to the left of the harbor. While the small handful of ships with people evident were heading to, or coming from, the right end of the water.

Anthony looked between the two ends of the harbor.

Polar opposite worlds.

Left was industrial and hard-hewn. The buildings were dark, simple, and lumbering, and seemed to go for miles.

To the right they were tall, sparkling in the half sun, beautiful and full of glass.

While everyone leaned and strained to see the city on the right, talking brightly about the new life they would have there, Anthony looked left curiously.

"Hold on. When you came here, The District didn't have any shipping anymore!" Olli protested. "The Great War was over by then. Everyone had moved—" she gestured behind her vaguely with her thumb in the general direction of the rest of Big Town, "and they didn't come all the way down to the docks for work anymore."

"It wasn't Razor shook his head. "There were still a couple of shipping companies."

Olli looked at him for a moment and tilted her head slightly. She stared at him for an extra beat before the corner of her eyes twitched. "I don't remember that."

"You <u>were</u> less than ten, Doll." Razor smirked slightly. "I doubt very much you were spending your time so completely engrossed in the inner workings of The District as you are now."

Olli gnawed on her lip a little. She grunted in an allowing way and nodded. "I guess that's a good point." She shifted slightly and looked at him curiously. "Which places?"

Razor shrugged. "I didn't ask. Honestly, it didn't seem all that strange to me at the time. It wasn't until I began to live here that I realized how dead The District really was."

Olli sucked on her teeth a little, looking completely lost in thought.

Razor cleared his throat and tilted his head.

Olli blinked a few times and focused on him. "Hm?"

"You <u>were</u> very little then. Honestly, I'd be surprised if you remembered something like that." He smiled at her and shook his head slightly. "I don't think <u>any</u> less of you."

Olli huffed a little and bobbed her head. "Right. Sorry. Go on."

Razor nodded a little and smirked. "You're going straight to that library upstairs when you get back to research, aren't you?"

Olli raised her eyebrows a little and tilted her head while she thought. "You're probably right," she allowed, a small smirk crossing her face.

Razor chuckled and nodded. "Just make sure to take a snack with you."

Olli looked at him for a moment and started to take a breath before she smirked and half laughed. "I'll make sure to do that." She shifted in her chair and adjusted her jacket behind the small of her back. "All right. I promise I'm done interrupting for a minute. What happened after the ship docked?"

Razor made a thoughtful noise and looked off into the middle distance.

Anthony glanced around him and took in the way that no one else looked toward the plain buildings. They made him curious.

Why were there so many ships coming from the side of the harbor that seemed to be...quiet.

He tilted his head a little and stepped over to nudge a man that was just a few feet from him. "What's the story, friend?" he wondered, half tilting his head toward the quieter side of the harbor.

The man shrugged and shook his head. "Sorry. My first time here."

Anthony smiled and half shook his head. "That's all right." He stepped back over to where he was standing and leaned against the railing loosely.

Seemed he was going to have to do his own investigating.

Chapter 4
The One With The Businessmen

"I know I said I wouldn't interrupt again soon..." Olli lightly scratched at her scalp a couple of seconds and pulled her lips back like she was wincing slightly. "I'm _really_ sorry. But I have another question."

Razor sighed and chuckled softly, looking at her in amusement. "And what would that be, Doll?"

"What made you choose Big Town? Why not Chicago, New York...Dallas is nice and warm, I hear..." Olli tilted her head.

"Weather isn't everything. If it was, I would have stayed in Sicily."

"Aces. Why _didn't_ you stay in Sicily?" Olli looked at him and her eyebrows jumped.

"That's a story for another day." Razor shook his head.

Olli made a protesting noise. "What? Why?!"

Razor looked at her and tilted his head. "You want me to stop this story and tell you why I left Sicily?"

"Well, no, not right _now_. But if this becomes a regular thing—"—Olli held up a hand—"which, I _really_ hope it doesn't." Olli looked at him dryly and shook her head a little when he made a protesting noise. "I want to have that story put on the docket."

Razor nodded. "All right."

"So." Olli cleared her throat and looked at him with a slight smile. "But really. Why did you choose Big Town when there's so many other places that you could have gone?" She scoffed a little. "You could have just stayed in Bay City. Or gone to South Town. It's not _that_ much further down the rail line."

Razor shrugged. "I guess it just called to me."

Olli tilted her head and made a thoughtful noise. "Is that so?"

Razor smirked. "Or maybe you should just sit back and let me tell the story and find out the organic way."

Olli clicked her tongue. "All right. Point taken. I'll try not to interrupt."

Razor chuckled. "It didn't take very long to dock..."

Anthony rested his right hip against the railing of the second deck and watched quietly as the ship got closed to the dock. He had opted to stay right where he was to keep from getting nearly crushed in the throng of people who were crowding to get to the lower deck and gangway.

He understood being eager to step foot onto American soil, but he wanted to take it all in. He had learned early on in his life the best way to survive was to make sure nothing was missed. Everything deserved a second look.

Sometimes a long one.

Watching people was entertaining, too.

Anthony smiled to himself and looked over the crowd, mentally updating the notes he took on his fellow passengers.

"What kind of notes?" Olli piped up.

Razor stood up and walked over to the dry bar and poured himself a drink. He looked over his left shoulder at her and shrugged. "Little, piddly things." He put the top back on the decanter and smiled at her a little as he walked back to the chair.

Olli watched him and raised her eyebrows. "You've been telling me an odyssean-level story with context and <u>amazing</u> in-depth detail that aren't important and <u>now</u> you tell me, '<u>little, piddly things</u>'?" She shook her head, smirking at him a bit.

Razor shrugged a bit. "I didn't think you would be bothered by my skipping over that detail to move the story along."

"Consider me interested." Olli shrugged.

Razor smirked and sipped his drink. "Are you sure I can't get you one of these? I feel rude drinking like this in front of you." He hefted his glass a little and tilted his head at her.

Olli shook her head without glassing at the glass. "No, thank you."

Razor clicked his tongue. "Come on, Doll."

Olli shook her head again. "I don't take drinks from strangers." She pursed her lips a little and shrugged. "I had a bad experience or two."

Razor made a soft, thoughtful noise and shrugged a little. "Maybe a little water?"

Olli shrugged. "I'm not thirsty. But thank you."

"You've been here for hours, Doll. I won't tell anyone." Razor shook his head slightly. "You must be thirsty."

Olli shook her head. "Nah. But thanks."

Razor looked at her for a moment and stood up again. He set his glass on the coaster near his pen well on the desk and brushed his hands off a little. "I notice little things. Things that make me good at what I do." He walked back to the dry bar and picked up a glass that looked like his.

Olli watched him and shifted in her chair to face him a little more square. "Mmmhm."

"Things like...who wears a wedding ring, but only when he's with his wife. Or who is dressed above their means because they're so desperate to be rich, they'll make their lives harder to impress people they don't even know. Or someone constantly fidgeting because there's a flask in their pocket that they've only just started to hide so it makes them nervous." He walked back to the desk and set the glass down where she could reach it if she so wished.

Olli made a noise of understanding. She watched him set down the glass and raised an eyebrow. "You're talking about things that a con man would notice."

Razor chuckled and shrugged a little. He walked around the edge of his desk and lightly dropped into his chair. "Or a good detective."

Olli smirked. "A fair point."

Razor shifted a little in his chair and adjusted his suit coat. "Water for you, Doll." He pointed to the glass in front of her on the desk.

Olli looked at the glass on the desk in front of her and smiled a little. "Thank you? But I'm really not thirsty."

Razor watched her and tilted his head. "I'm not going to drug you."

Olli glanced at the water and then back at him. "No, thanks."

"Suit yourself." Razor shrugged a little, unruffled by the brush-off. "All right. Continuing on."

Olli nodded. "Go ahead."

Anthony switched his gaze to the workers on the dock. Busy bees, the whole lot of them.

There they were, throwing lines, tying knots and hurling short sentences back and forth at each other. It seemed like they would crash into each other at any moment, but the collision never happened. A couple of men were busy just under the roofed walkway, setting up a half dozen tables, the same number of uniformed men standing close, eyeing them.

Anthony tilted his head a little and focused on the uniformed men. He pondered them for a moment, trying to fathom out who they were.

"Customs agents?" Olli assumed, not even bothering to look apologetic for the interruption.

Razor nodded. "Exactly."

"Had you not prepared for that? Trying to sneak in some pasta sauce?" Olli raised her eyebrow slightly.

Razor laughed and made a humming noise as he sighed. "Ah, Doll, I never lack for entertainment while you're around."

Olli smirked in a brilliant way and shrugged. "I do what I can. Seriously though. Did you not think about customs?"

"I wasn't worried. Just didn't expect such a show of force."

"It's a big port. They handle over three ships a day currently. And I hear numbers are <u>down</u> since ten years ago." Olli tilted her head. "Why were you surprised there were so many customs agents?"

Razor chuckled quietly. "You sell me so short."

Olli raised her eyebrows a little and scoffed. "I'm sure I do. Tell me."

"I was actually really rather impressed with how efficient they were."

Olli made a half-interested noise and smiled a little. "Ah. Makes sense." She swirled her hand around a little. "All right, so you docked. They funneled everyone off the boat and got them through customs. You got your passport stamped—"

"I'm confused. Are you telling this story? Or am I?" Razor tilted his head.

"Just trying to get you back up to speed. Consider it a push-start." Olli smirked.

Razor rolled his eyes and shook his head a little. "Thank you for that."

Olli grinned at him brilliantly.

"It was actually while I was standing in line that I first heard about a businessman in the next town over that was looking to invest some money..."

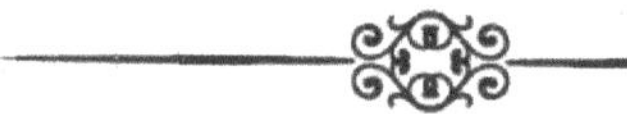

Anthony stood where he was on the upper deck, leaning against the railing, watching the stream of people work their way off the ship in pairs down the gangway. Once they were off the ship, some pairs would stick together and walk to a table. Others would group up into their families to line up in front of a table.

He had opted to stay on the second deck as long as possible, so he didn't have to be in the throng. It was always better to wait for a bit when the line was a few hours long. Plus, it gave him time to people watch a bit more.

It was almost an hour later before Anthony bent down to pick up the leather edged, locked suitcase that had been resting against his calf between his right leg and the low wall that he had been leaning on. Anthony put a soft brown fedora on his head as he walked to the staircase between him and the main deck.

He didn't hurry down the steps. The line was still incredibly long. He had plenty of time to kill before he even set foot on the gangway.

Plus, there wasn't really anything that was worse than the hurry-up-and-wait game.

Anthony saunter-stepped onto the main deck and meandered toward where the line turned more into a pool of people milling around waiting for their turn down the gangway. He nodded and smiled at a couple of people he had interacted with a bit while on the trip over. He scooped a carpetbag away from a tired mother and entrusted it to her teenage son with a pointed look in his direction.

A quick peck to her cheek and a soft hair scrub for the toddler on her hip, he continued on.

Once he found a place that was a bit out of the way again, he settled into wait. He sat down in a wire wrapped metal chair next to a tea table and set his suitcase under the table.

Here was as good a place to wait as any. He wished for an espresso. Or maybe a glass of wine. Something to sip while he waited for the crowd to thin out.

Anthony looked around quietly, people watching again. It was a wonderful way to pass the time. Even with nothing to sip on.

There were a couple of men over to his right that caught his attention. He didn't remember seeing them during the week-long trip. Which didn't mean all that much, just happened to miss each other, he was sure.

Businessmen that probably were coming here to America to make some sort of deal.

"...I'm telling you. He has more money than he knows what to do with, and he's looking for some business opportunities."

"And he's in the next town over?"

"He runs the whole warehouse district. They say that he's got a string of clubs. You can buy every kind of gin you want. Girls, too. Man's not just practically above the law; he _is_ the law in town, I hear."

"A regular Al Capone, eh?"

Anthony's eyebrow went up a little, and he glanced at them past the very edge of the brim of his fedora.

Not the businessmen he had pegged them for.

How very interesting—

Chapter 5
The One With The Temporary Friends

Anthony stood up, not the least bit in a hurry. He picked up his fedora and dropped it on his head, after bending down and scooping up his suitcase. He wandered toward the tail end of the line, accidentally-on-purpose ending up within close earshot of the two con men that were still discussing their mark.

"Wait!"

"Yes, Doll?" Razor tilted his head. "What would you like to ask?"

"How did you know?"

"How did I know what?"

"They were con men?" Olli's eyebrow jumped up fractionally.

"Did you not hear what they said?" Razor tilted his head.

"Sure. But, Aces Razor, they could have just been a couple of salesmen." Olli shrugged. "Salesmen tend to talk about people with money looking for investments." She shook her head again and adjusted in her chair. "Not to mention the fact that ten—fifteen years ago there were <u>plenty</u> of men with a lot of money and thought they ran Big Town with or without the police's say-so."

Razor pursed his lips a little and shook his head. "No. There's a difference. You know what they say. Takes one to know one."

Olli nodded a little. "Fair enough."

Razor pointed to the water again. "If I drink some of it first, will you at least take a sip?"

Olli shrugged. "I'm really not thirsty."

Razor sighed a little and nodded. "All right. Where was I?"

"In line. Listening to a couple of bad con men talking about a rich businessman here in Big Town that was above the law."

Razor nodded and touched his nose. "That's right. Thank you."

"Glad I could help." Olli smirked and leaned into her chair comfortably.

Anthony listened casually as they moved their way to the gangway. He made sure he let a couple exit the ship before he stepped off, creating a buffer between him and the con men.

No need to let them know he was listening in.

He was incredibly curious.

Who could they be after?

And why did they feel comfortable enough to talk about it so openly?

He couldn't decide if he was <u>impressed</u> with their bravery, or astounded by their <u>stupidity</u>.

"That does seem strange..." Olli mused, her tone thoughtfully quiet. "Like a rookie mistake."

Razor grunted. "Or that of men who thought that no one was listening."

"People are <u>always</u> listening," Olli protested.

Razor made a noise of agreement. "It's true, you never know when someone might be listening." He shrugged. "They didn't perceive me, or anyone else around them, as a threat."

"Clearly they weren't looking," Olli smirked at him.

Razor chuckled. "Thank you?"

Olli shook her head. She smirked a little and shifted in her chair. "Sorry. I interrupted again."

Razor shrugged. "I followed them off the ship..."

Anthony stepped off the gangway and set foot on American soil for the first time in his life.

For the moment, he was glad the line wasn't moving forward too quickly. He wanted a moment to enjoy the feeling of succeeding in completing a goal that he had set for himself years before.

It was a good feeling.

He looked around and walked after the two of men again. He found it odd they talked so openly about their plans.

Perhaps they were hoping most people around them would be so excited to be in America they wouldn't be noticed or heard.

Or perhaps they assumed they wouldn't know anything about what they were talking about. It still seemed a bit brazen though.

Anthony moved forward a few steps at a time as the line progressed past the customs agents and their guards.

He offered his papers to the liveried officer behind the table three over and one behind the table the con men stopped at. Anthony set his suitcase on the table and smiled charmingly. He glanced over to see where they were while his suitcase was open. He nodded once at the man across the table from him and swung his hands behind his hips to hold them there while he waited.

So far the two men were all moving at about the same pace.

Which was good.

He didn't want to hurry up to catch up with them, but there was no way he was going to lose them.

Curiosity had completely taken over at this point.

"You're all set."

Anthony turned his attention back to the man on the other side of the table and smiled brightly. "Thank you. Very much." He grabbed the handle of his suitcase. "Have a wonderful day." He smiled brightly.

"You as well," was the wooden response.

Anthony picked up the suitcase and walked around the table. He adjusted the fedora on his head and made his way to the exit, just like the dozens of people around him. Though, those around him weren't deliberately trying to make sure they ended up in the crowd where they did.

Anthony had placed himself in the crowd right where he wanted to be. Here he could hear everything that the con men said to each other, but would be far enough away to avoid them noticing he was following them.

No reason to make them stop talking.

It was <u>always</u> a good idea to be well informed.

"And by well informed, you mean you never know when you might be able to scoop them." Olli wondered, tilting her head slightly.

Razor made a thoughtful noise. "You know...that's a very good way to put it."

Olli scoffed.

It was only a couple of minutes worth of walking to leave the dock behind and walk out onto a crowded concrete pad. People were milling around, looking at the buildings of their new city.

Some people were walking toward the road, already comfortable enough that they apparently knew where they were going. There were some people hugging friends or relatives, excited to meet up with people they hadn't seen in years or decades.

Anthony moved through the crowd, a few feet off and parallel to the men. He looked around a little, taking in the buildings and the added people. He wasn't sure why he was surprised that somehow it was the same sort of feeling as the port they had left the week before.

After all, people are people, no matter where they were.

Anthony looked across the half dozen paces to the right that separated him from the con men he had been following.

Apparently, they had absolutely no clue he was following them.

Not very bright, these two.

Must not have gotten into much trouble back home.

Anthony walked after them, spending most of his time looking around where they were going, only checking in with them every-so-often to make sure he didn't get left behind. He wondered idly if he had ever crossed their paths before. They didn't look very familiar. But then again, he had seen a lot of people. And they had looked in his direction a few times. It didn't appear that they recognized him either.

Which was <u>probably</u> for the best.

Unlike everyone else fresh off the ship, they were walking more toward the edge of town. Not toward town center.

Where were they going?

Anthony finally ran out of the medium-sized crowd he was using as a buffer. He walked along behind them, making sure to keep his body language just like theirs.

They lead him directly to the train station.

Anthony looked around at the station.

Who stepped off a boat and walked directly onto a train?

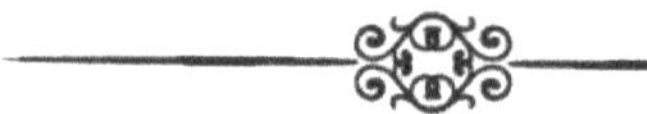

"They must have been heading for Big Town. Passenger ships always port at Bay City. Even <u>before</u> The District was The District." Olli sat up a little and leaned forward to rest her forearms on her knees, completely enthralled. "Al told me it was because there wasn't room for passengers <u>and</u> industry on this side of The Harbor."

Razor nodded. "I've been told."

"Did it seem like they had been here before?" Olli tilted her head. "Have you seen them since?"

Razor held up a hand. "Slow down there, Doll."

"Right. Aces. Go on."

Anthony walked into the train station after his leaders, too curious not to see it through at this point. He stopped at a newsstand near the ticket takers. He paid the man running the stand while listening for where his friends were going.

He checked to see their progress in line. They had only moved up a couple of places in line. Apparently, the person taking money in exchange for tickets wasn't in much of a hurry.

It didn't look like they were either. They were smiling and chatting with each other like they had all the time in the world.

Anthony smiled at the man running the stand and folded the newspaper in half, before stuffing it under his left arm, right up under his shoulder. Once he had it pinned there where he could hold it, Anthony fished in his pocket and offered the money the young boy running the newsstand requested. He picked up his suitcase and walked over to the line.

At this point, he was quite sure that they didn't care, even _if_ they thought he was following them.

That didn't mean he was going to crowd them too much.

Anthony meandered to a stop at the end of the line, just a few paces from his quarry. He set the suitcase down at his feet, pulled the paper from between his arms and his ribs, and flipped it open.

Appearing to read the paper gave him more of a chance to listen to the conversations around him. It was amazing to him how people would talk when they didn't think anyone was close enough to hear.

Or, even worse, if they considered the person too busy to actually be listening in.

Anthony waited about as long as he thought he could draw it out and flipped the paper, without opening it, to look like he was reading under the fold.

The men in front of him must have run out of things to talk about. They stood and looked at the line in front of them like they were wondering if it was ever going to move.

Anthony smiled a little to himself and took the opportunity to step a little closer to them when the line finally moved for the first time after he got into it.

It was a long shot, but if he could get them talking about their pitch, maybe he could figure out who they were going to meet. Maybe he had the chance to make some walking around money now that he was Stateside.

And if they were too rude, or blew him off, he'd weasel the name of the mark they were after out of them and just...beat them to the punch somehow.

Anthony looked up and picked up his suitcase. He stepped forward two steps and then another half as the line moved.

It was time to make some new, temporary friends.

Chapter 6
The One With The Third Platform

Anthony stood in line for a few more minutes and stepped forward a couple more steps when it moved again.

Never in his life had a line moved so slow. The line to get on the ship to come to America was nearly triple the size of this line, and he had stepped onto the ship _much_ faster than he was moving through this line.

Now that he had made up his mind, and was closer to the con men in front of him, he was content to use the paper in the way it had been intended. He opened it and simply started with the first article at the top left corner.

Anthony folded down the corner a bit to see what was happening when he heard boots scuff.

It was about time that the line started to move again. He had just started to wonder if it ever would.

He folded the paper back together and then in half. He folded it in half again and stuffed it under his arm. Apparently, something had changed behind the brass bars in the ticket taker booth.

Five people had gone through the line already. It had only been a few minutes.

Anthony looked at the ticket taker and nodded a little to himself.

It made more sense now.

There had been a shift change.

The man taking money and doling out tickets was different than the one just ten minutes before. He apparently took his job _much_ more seriously than his counterpart. He was waving the next person in line forward as he was instructing the person with a new ticket where they were supposed to go.

He stepped forward again as the line moved.

Time to start working his plan.

"Thank goodness. I was starting to wonder if I was going to be stuck in this line forever." Anthony mused, making sure his tone was travel weary, frustrated, and relieved all at the same time.

The two men in front of him scoffed and made some sort of agreeing noise.

"We were wondering if we were going to miss out on all the trains for the day," the man on the left spoke up, his tone not much different than Anthony's.

Anthony chuckled and nodded.

"Where you heading to?" The man on the right wondered, pivoting a little to join the conversation.

Anthony shrugged. "Nowhere special. What about you gents?"

The three of them all stepped forward a couple of steps to keep up with the movement of the line.

"We've got business the next town over."

Razor smiled and nodded. "Business good then?"

They stepped forward a few more steps as the line moved again.

"You just get in?" the man on the left wondered, looking at Anthony. "I saw you on the ship earlier today."

"Oh yeah. Look at that. You were on the ship!"

"Back actually." Anthony shrugged. "How long are you here for?"

"We'll only be here for a couple of weeks and then we're on the boat back to Italy."

"Good gracious. That's quite the tight timetable." Anthony mused, blinking and looking surprised.

The man on the right nodded. "We don't have a lot of time, unfortunately."

They took a few more steps forward and paused. Now they were only a couple of steps from the ticket taker.

"Must be some deal if you're willing to spend two weeks on the ocean. Especially within a three-week window." Anthony smirked.

The men laughed and nodded a little. "You know how it is. Gotta make the money to bring it back home."

Anthony nodded and made a noise of agreement. "I can understand that."

"What about you?" the man on the right wondered. "You said you're back. Got a place around here then?"

Anthony shook his head. "Just been here a couple of times." He shrugged, playing it off like it wasn't something to talk about.

Olli held up a hand. "I have a question."

Razor looked at her and tilted his head. "Yes, Doll?"

"You've been here before?" Olli tilted her head, the first finger of the hand that was up pointing toward the floor.

"This _is_ my office." Razor gestured around a little. "I'm here basically every day, nearly all day long."

Olli's shoulders dropped, her hand fell into her lap in a flop, and she looked at him for a moment like she had lost all of her mental energy.

Razor chuckled and smirked. "I take it you're talking more about me being here in the States before that trip?"

Olli pursed her lips for a moment and then nodded. "Yeah. That's what I was talking about."

Razor shook his head a little. "No. Came up with it on the fly. Worked in my favor."

"So you lied. And then had to keep the lie up the whole time you were with them."

"Olli...you've literally described what it is that con man does." Razor looked at her and raised an eyebrow slightly.

Olli blew out a small breath and nodded a little. "Right. You're right. Sorry. Go on."

"Did you forget for a second?" Razor wondered, chuckling softly.

Olli shrugged and half rolled her eyes. "Aces. Maybe."

Razor chuckled some more and adjusted how he was sitting. "All right. So. We finally got up to the ticket window..."

"Destination?" The plump, alert man behind the brass bars wondered, pinning the man to Anthony's right with an expectant look.

"Big Town please?"

The man nodded and pressed a small button in front of him. There was a loud shunktd noise and a crisp ticket appeared out of a small slit near his right hand. "Three-fifty."

Once the money and ticket were exchanged, the man stepped away from the window, holding his ticket and smiling a little. He paused slightly and waited for his companion to buy a ticket.

Anthony held back as they bought their tickets and nodded once in a friendly way when they glanced at him before walking off. He stepped up to the window and smiled charmingly.

"Destination?" the man behind the bars wondered, not sounding the least bit bored with the same question.

"When does the next train for Big Town leave?" Anthony wondered, smiling in a charming way.

"Thirty minutes."

"Wonderful. Could I have a ticket please?"

"Three-fifty." The man nodded, pushing the button to call another single ticket from the deep vault.

Anthony dug out his wallet and nodded. "Thank you. So much." He offered the money and took the ticket when it was offered to him. "Which platform?"

"That would be platform three. Down the main hall there and to the left." The man pointed to his right with the practice of countless times gesturing the same way.

Anthony smiled at him brightly and nodded. "Thank you very much. Have a wonderful day."

"Yeah. You too. Next?" The man behind the bars waved the next customer over, already disconnected from the conversation he had with Anthony.

Anthony bent down and scooped up his suitcase before turning and walking the direction of the main hallway he had been pointed to. He wandered down the hall, not in too much of a hurry. Bumping into his marks would take some careful planning.

Accidentally-on-purpose took a lot more finesse than it appeared to be.

Run into them too soon, and they would begin to think he was looking for them.

But not finding them in time meant risking losing them when they reached Big Town.

Anthony stopped at a stand and picked up a map. A quick look told him what he thought was true.

Big Town was large.

Looked like it would be large enough to easily lose track of someone quickly the moment they stepped off the train. He refolded the map up and set it back in the holder.

At the bottom of the hallway was a large portico, feeding off into three platforms on this side of the station. A small cart sat directly in the middle, selling pastries and coffee to travelers waiting for their trains.

Anthony looked around slowly, looking for the two men he was following. For the moment, it looked like they were sitting on a bench near the entrance to platform three. Looked like they had picked up a couple of newspapers, and one of them was holding a powdery looking pastry in one hand.

Good.

If they were relaxed enough to read the paper, then they were none the wiser they being followed.

Anthony walked up to the cart and smiled brightly. "Good afternoon! Just a coffee please?" he dug into his pocket for some change that had wormed its way to the bottom of his pocket.

The man nodded quietly and poured a cup quickly. "Two cents."

Anthony pulled his hand out of his pocket and sifted through the change for a moment before dropping a nickel in the man's palm. "Keep the change. Thank you so much." He took the paper cup carefully and smiled brightly. After scooping up his suitcase again, Anthony walked away from the coffee cart in the general direction of platform three. He found a concrete bench under one of the soaring columns that held up the lofty ceiling and sat down carefully.

He had about twenty minutes before he needed to meet his train. Plenty of time to reach the platform and 'bump' into his new friends.

Chapter 7
The One With The Game

A sharp whistle echoed through the station.

A swoop-nosed, streamlined locomotive chugged slowly into platform three. Steam escaping from around the wheels, blowing hot clouds past the few souls brave enough to crowd the near edge where the platform met the rails.

Anthony stepped onto the main part of the platform just a few dozen steps behind his quarry. He looked at the train and smiled.

It looked brand new and like it had been polished recently. No more heavy, half century old engines like back home.

America was starting to shape up to be an amazing place.

The train chugged along the platform, its pace almost excruciatingly slow. Car after car clacked past, finally coming to a stop only when the first car was just about to leave the station and enter the outside world again. When the train finally stopped moving, the first door on the first car was perfectly in line with the end of the platform.

Almost like a magician, the conductor stepped out of the first car, through the steam, only missing a top hat and a cape to swish. He walked the length of the train, opening doors and letting people off as he went.

The mob of afternoon travelers poured off the train cars. Most were businessmen, apparently on their way home from work. It seemed everyone was carrying a briefcase of some sort. They walked past the crowd waiting for the train, almost like they didn't see any of them. All of their focus was on the hall that led up to the main terminal and the outside world.

Every eye trained on the hanging metal sign with an arrow. On it, painted in large, gold and black beautiful lettering:

Bay City

Anthony watched them go, keeping half an eye on the two men he had trailed here. No one paid him any mind, and that was fine with him.

The two men walked into the fourth car in line, chatting together like old chums.

Anthony made his way through the crowd, pulling the paper out from between his arm and ribs, holding it in his free hand as he walked. He passed the fourth car, and the fifth. He didn't slow down until he reached the seventh car.

Up three big steps and he looked to his right.

The car was modest, but beautifully clean. Bright blues and greens. With gold trim on every accent. It wasn't a first-class car, but it wasn't the worst he had ever seen.

Anthony walked halfway down the car and set his suitcase next to a bench seat. He sat down closest to the window, pulled his hat off his head and set it on his suitcase. The paper sat on his lap for a moment while Anthony looked out of the window. There wasn't much to see, but he was curious for a split second.

He blinked and turned his attention to the paper in his lap. After picking it up, he crossed one leg over the other and opened the paper to the first page. As long as he had a little time to kill, he might as well read the paper that he bought while he waited for the train to leave.

<u>Actually</u> read it this time. Not just pretend to while he listened in on the conversations around him.

People filtered into the car, conversations bouncing between them. A few greeted each other like they had done it a million times on this same train, at this same time, every day.

Anthony ignored the conversations and read his paper.

It was only a few minutes later when the sharp whistle squealed.

The conductor was out on the platform bellowing it was the final chance to get aboard before the train left.

A few more people charged onto the train, dropping and crowding into seats and chatting with people around them.

The train car jerked roughly a few moments later. It seemed to stay in limbo between a forward and backward motion before it started to inch forward.

Anthony folded his paper toward himself and looked out the window to see the last of the city as the train started to slowly move out toward the city limits. It didn't look much different than some of the cities back home. The buildings were a little different, but the feel was the same. People lived here. They worked here. Fell in love. Started families.

Anthony smiled a little to himself and looked over the people in his car that he could see. There was something comforting about how familiar this all was.

About fifteen minutes down the track, a liveried conductor in bright blues and silver accents walked down the car, pausing at each seat, requesting tickets.

Anthony pulled out his ticket and offered it to the conductor when he arrived at his seat.

"Ticket?" The conductor smiled and took the ticket. He punched a small hole in the top edge and offered it back. "Thanks for riding with us today."

Anthony smiled and took the ticket. "Thank you. How long of a trip is it to Big Town?"

"Another half hour, sir."

Anthony smiled and nodded. "Thank you." He folded up his paper and rested back in his seat. A half hour didn't leave him a whole lot of time to spend with his new friends that didn't know they were friends.

Perhaps that was better, anyway.

About ten minutes later, Anthony picked up his hat, newspaper, and suitcase. He stepped past the two men sitting near him and walked toward the doorway that would lead him to the next car.

Walking through the next couple of cars took him almost no time at all.

Anthony stepped into the fourth car and gently, but firmly, pulled the door closed behind him. He looked around the car, trying to track down his marks. It only took a couple of seconds to find them.

It wasn't like they were hiding.

They had no idea what was stalking them.

Anthony walked forward a few more seats and settled himself down in an empty spot where he could see his prey. They were only two seats away and on the other side of the aisle. He would be able to watch them from here until they noticed him. Anthony pulled his hat off his head and set it down on the top edge of his suitcase.

The paper was opened next, though this time he refolded it so it was folded back on itself so he could hold it one hand.

But most importantly, his face was visible.

Anthony shifted in his seat a bit and settled himself in to wait for his queries to notice him. He checked his watch. Still twenty-five minutes left before he had to worry about bumping into them as they got off the train.

That would make this play a little more difficult.

Didn't mean that it couldn't be <u>done.</u> Just that it would be a bit more tricky.

He enjoyed a challenge, but working two con men was challenge enough. As a general rule, con men were inherently more skeptical than most.

But he was in the correct car to make the play now. And that was what mattered. The game was afoot, and he was ready to play.

Chapter 8
The One With The Gangster

"Hey!"

Anthony raised his eyebrows slightly and finished the line he was reading, and looked up. "Me?" he wondered innocently.

The man that had been on his right in line for a ticket nodded and smiled a little. "Yeah. You were in line behind us, weren't you? For a ticket."

Anthony looked at him for a moment, feigning confusion and searching his memory for his face. He smiled a little and nodded. "Oh! That's right. I did see you there. We talked about how long the line was taking to move."

The man that had been on his left sat forward a little and looked back at him over his shoulder and around the corner of his seat. "Well! Hello there!"

Anthony smiled. "Hello."

"Come on over here. Come here! Have a seat. It's a train, not your chair by the fire at home. Read the paper later. Come chat."

Anthony looked at his paper and back up to them. He nodded a little and started to gather his things. "If you insist."

They both smiled and waved him over toward them. One even moved closer to the window and left a space open for him.

"Come. Sit."

Anthony scooped up the handle of his suitcase and stood up. He walked the two seats up and stepped to his left to sit. "Well, thank you."

"What's your name, Mack?"

"Anthony."

"You told them your <u>real</u> name?!" Olli's voice jumped two octaves and cracked.

Razor looked at her for a moment and shrugged. "I wasn't going to see them ever again."

Olli's eyebrows jumped a little, and she tilted her head. "But you still...your <u>real</u> name."

"You know my real name. I fail to see the consequences?"

"You didn't tell me your name." Olli shrugged. "I didn't think you told anyone your real name."

Razor half bobbed his head. "I did every so often. Otherwise, it wouldn't be in those reports that you read to <u>learn</u> my name."

"Just to keep things interesting?" Olli assumed, tilting her head slightly.

Razor grunted. "Something like that." He shrugged a little. "Shall I continue?"

Olli nodded. "Yeah. Go ahead."

"Anthony. Nice to meet you." the man across from him spoke first. "Eddy," he pointed to himself. "And that's Teo." He gestured to the man that was sitting next to Anthony.

"Think those were their real names?" Olli wondered, tilting her head.

Razor's shoulders dropped a little and he looked at her like she was trying his patience. "I don't know."

"You couldn't tell?" Olli's eyebrows jumped slightly. "That doesn't sound like you."

"I've been lied to before." Razor smirked. "And have even been fooled a few times."

Olli dropped back in her chair and looked at him for a moment, like she couldn't process what he was saying.

Razor smirked and chuckled a little. "Oh, come now. You didn't think I was invincible, did you?"

Olli frowned a little. "You've been conned before?"

Razor bobbed his head and looked a little confused. "It's happened to everyone at one point or another, Doll."

Olli grunted a little. "Sure..."

"And frankly, I didn't really care if they gave me their real names or not."

A thoughtful look crossed Olli's face and she shrugged a little. "I guess that makes sense."

"But. What I _can_ tell you is that they did not feel the least bit worried about me. They were very chatty and friendly."

Olli tented her fingers and rested her elbows on the arms of her chair. "Go on."

"Nice to meet you both, gents." Anthony smiled at them brightly. "So you're off to Big Town! What are you two doing there?"

"We're meeting up with a big wig with a lot of money to burn. We're going to get him to invest in our restaurant," Teo smirked.

"A restaurant?" Anthony smiled, looking at him curiously. "What kind?"

Eddy shifted a little and opened the briefcase, and offered Anthony a simple folder that had a small stack of papers inside. "Here's our proposal."

Anthony took the folder and looked a little stunned. "You are incredibly well organized. I wasn't expecting this." He smiled and opened the file. "An Italian place..."

"Wait." Olli sat up a little straighter. "_Wait_." She pursed her lips and started to take a breath before shaking her head.

"Yes?"

"They just...handed over the folded like it was nothing!"

"They were businessmen. I looked like one of them. Business-men have no issue handing over plans. It's not like I would steal them." He smirked. "At least. As far as they <u>knew</u>."

"You were going to steal their business plan?" Olli tilted her head.

Razor wrinkled his nose and tutted a bit. "Good gracious, no. I planned to steal their <u>mark</u>."

"<u>That</u> makes sense." Olli hummed a little in her throat and bobbed her head. "All right. I'm tracking. Go on."

"Just how Nona makes it." Teo smiled brightly.

Anthony made a thoughtful noise and turned a few pages. "He must be from home if you keep using references like this." He tapped a line in the pages he was reading.

Teo and Eddy both chuckled the same time he did.

"We hear he's a second generation. He has a Nona in the old country. So we figured he'd want to bring a little bit of home over here."

Anthony made a half-interested noise and flipped the next page. "I must say it seems very well thought out." He smiled and offered Eddy the folder back with a warm smile. "I'm sure he'll be very impressed."

"That's the plan." Teo agreed, a bright smile crossing his face.

"Are you going to be working with your investor, then?" Anthony asked before looking up at both of them, "Or are you just selling him on the idea and letting him run with it?" Anthony wondered, addressing Teo. Feeding into his want to be the important one in the conversation, before looking back down at the file in his hands.

"Aces, hold on..." Olli protested, holding up a hand. "I know you're good, but how could you possibly know that he wanted to be the most important one in the conversation?"

Razor smirked a little and shrugged. "It was the way he volunteered information. Almost like he had been holding onto it until it was the perfect time to achieve maximum..." Razor paused for a moment. "Good impression? For lack of a better explanation."

Olli thought about it for a moment and grunted. "Sure. I understand that."

Razor smirked. "So, I fed into it."

"Of course you did. You're a proper con man." Olli smirked.

Teo preened a little and looked pleased that he had been consulted. "We were thinking a more hands off approach." He gestured toward the file in Eddy's hand. "We're just selling the man on the idea."

Anthony nodded and smiled a little. "I see. You're not even going to be around to help set up this idea in its physical capacity?" He looked at Eddy for a moment and then back at Teo."

"We're still trying to decide that." Eddy shrugged.

"I don't think that it's a good idea. Eddy wants to be helpful." Teo scoffed a little and pointed at Eddy a little, like he thought it a joke.

Eddy looked slightly irritated and frowned.

Anthony nodded a little and made a thoughtful noise. "Think he's got the acumen to start up a restaurant without any assistance from the two of you?"

Eddy shook his head. "No—"

"Of _course_ he will be able to!" Teo protested, cutting Eddy off. "The man has dozens of nightclubs."

Eddy frowned again. "You don't know that. It's just rumor."

"Rumor is often found to be following truth!" Teo pointed out, almost immediately.

Anthony looked between the two of them. "Rumor of how many nightclubs again?" He focused on Teo.

Teo smiled like a hungry shark. "Dozens."

"Dozens?" Anthony mused, shock coloring his words. He laughed a little. "Sounds like you're going after a _gangster_." He looked between the two of them. "You're not..._actually_ going after a _gangster_?"

Eddy looked at Teo and frowned a little.

Anthony caught the look. "No..."

Teo shook his head. "He's a businessman!"

"Dozens of nightclubs," Eddy pointed out skeptically.

"What's this gangster's name?" Anthony wondered, still looking like he didn't believe it for a second and was just giving them a good-natured ribbing.

"Joey."

"Joey. See? Hardly scary at all." Teo smirked.

"Joey." Anthony chuckled and shook his head. "No. He does not."

"Joey <u>Leftfoot</u>." Eddy repeated, looking at Teo like he was imploring him to take the name and implications seriously.

"Joey <u>Leftfoot</u>." Anthony repeated, tilting his head and knitting his eyebrows. "<u>Joey Leftfoot</u>?!"

Chapter 9
The One With The Poor Planning

"You <u>knew</u> that he was a gangster and jumped on the bandwagon anyway?!" Olli looked at him like she thought he was absolutely insane. She waved her hand a little. "Wait! <u>No</u>. I have a better question."

Razor sipped his drink and tilted his head. "What would that be?"

"How did you <u>know</u> he was a gangster?" Olli's eyebrow tilted a little, and she looked at him closely. "Was he in the papers back in Italy or something?"

Razor chuckled and shook his head a little. "Good gracious <u>no</u>. I just happened to read an article in the paper that I had bought in Bay City."

Olli made a thoughtful noise and bobbed her head a little. "<u>That</u> makes a little more sense." She tapped her chin a little with a couple of fingers. "Again...you knew he was a gangster. And you still jumped in with both feet."

Razor shrugged. "He's a gangster, not a god. He's just a man."

Olli's eyebrows jumped, and she scoffed. "I see."

Razor smirked.

"You don't have to look <u>so</u> proud," Olli scolded.

"I'm afraid that particular feeling is not one I am capable of controlling." Razor smirked, the pride not dimming at all at Olli's scolding.

Olli looked at him for a moment and shook her head. "Aces. All right." She waved a hand, the other one held up in a steadying motion. "Sorry I asked. What happened next?"

Anthony leaned back against his seat and looked between the two of them. He folded his arms over his chest and tilted his head. "You're going to work over a <u>gangster</u>."

Eddy swallowed a little and pursed his lips, clearly uncomfortable with the information. He didn't look thrilled at the prospect.

"With <u>this</u>?" Anthony shook the file a little bit, every movement he made skeptical.

"So this Eddy wasn't the one who came up with the idea...Teo had managed to convince him it was a good idea before you crossed their paths," Olli summed up, tilting her head slightly.

Razor nodded a little and grunted. "Confirming what I had thought already. Teo seemed like the brains of the operation."

"The con part of the operation or the business idea part of the operation?" Olli tilted her head slightly.

Razor looked brightly proud and tapped his nose. "Clever girl." He smiled and chuckled quietly. "A little bit of both actually, I assumed."

"So naturally, he's the one you focused on." Olli smirked.

Teo scoffed and shook his head a little. "No."

Anthony looked at him and his eyebrow inched up fractionally. "Beg pardon?"

Teo waved his hand a little. "We're not going there to <u>talk</u> to the gangster." He looked at Eddy and shook his head again. "We're going to talk to the man that owns a few clubs and might be interested in buying another one." He reached forward and pulled the file away from Anthony, almost like a parent snatching something away from their child.

Anthony held up his hand and smiled in a charming way.

Eddy didn't look convinced and glanced at Anthony, trying to gauge his reaction, hoping to pick up his support.

Anthony made a thoughtful noise. "You think he's going to separate them?"

Teo shrugged and brushed off the comment with a few swings of his hand, seemingly wiping away the concern. "It's all under control."

Eddy looked at Anthony and then back at Teo. "This is a terrible plan."

"It is not! Eddy! Have I ever steered you wrong?" Teo scoffed.

Eddy looked at Anthony again and pursed his lips.

Anthony chuckled. "All right. I have to know. How did this get started?" He chuckled, scooping his hat off and setting it on his knee after crossing one over the other. "What possessed you to go after a gangster with a few clubs instead of a different business-man? Maybe one that's a little less dangerous?"

Teo shook his head. "Nah. We're just selling an idea. He doesn't have to buy it. And it's not like we're selling him a building that actually exists!"

Anthony chuckled and nodded a little. "All right. I suppose that's a fair point. Does he know you're coming?"

Eddy looked at Teo, clearly not sure of the answer.

Teo shrugged a little. "I'm not sure."

"You're not sure." Anthony chuckled. "You are a brave man, Sir."

"Do you even know where he's going to be?" Eddy wondered, looking at Teo sharply.

Teo shrugged a little. "We'll start with the most popular clubs and work our way around."

Eddy didn't seem to like the answer. He looked over at Anthony and blinked a couple of times like he wasn't sure how to process the information. He looked at Teo and shook his head, completely dissatisfied.

Anthony cleared his throat a little. He looked between them and smiled warmly. "Hey. We've still got some time before we get to where we need to be. What do you say we talk about something that isn't business?" he looked between them again and smiled softly. "Tell me about home."

Olli cleared her throat and tilted her head slightly.

"You have a question?" Razor assumed, using the break in the story to take a sip of his drink.

Olli nodded a bit and smiled. "What did you think of that information?"

"What information?" Razor tilted his head.

"The fact that this Teo..." Olli's hand flipped around a couple of times like she was trying to come up with the right word for what she was trying to explain. "Didn't have a plan on how to find Joey, much less let him know they were coming?"

"Ahhhhhhh." Razor nodded a little and grunted. "I wasn't a fan. I thought it was a rather risky move as it was, trying to get him to buy into an idea that wasn't proved. But...fortune favors the bold I suppose."

Olli nodded a little. "But...the plan to find him?" She shook her head. "I thought it was a little strange at best."

Razor shrugged a bit. "I don't know what to tell you. I thought they were going to be more planned out, based on the proposal that I flipped through."

Olli looked thoughtful for a moment, gnawing on the inside left corner of her bottom lip.

"What is it?" Razor looked at her, smirking like he knew she had something good.

Olli started to take a breath. She shook her head a little and cleared her throat. "Did...do you think Eddy knew it was a con?"

Razor looked at her for a moment. "What do you mean?"

"It seems to me...from the way you're talking about it...Teo is running a con. Eddy has no idea what's <u>actually</u> is going on." Olli shrugged a little and tilted her head.

Razor didn't move for a moment and tilted his head, clearly considering what she had said. "You know...I hadn't really considered it until now."

Olli's eyebrows jumped a little and she tilted her head. "You didn't consider it?"

Razor shrugged again. "I didn't really need to at the moment."

"Just because you didn't need it doesn't seem like you would <u>discount</u> it either."

Razor shrugged a little and smiled in a small way. "Sorry, Doll. Can't think of everything. And at the time, I hadn't really thought it worth noting. I wasn't going to see them ever again."

Olli grunted and bobbed her head. "All right...sorry. Go on. Tell me what happened next."

"It's really boring."

Olli dropped her head back against the headrest of the chair. "Somehow, I feel like that isn't the least bit true."

Razor smirked and chuckled. "Honest, Doll, the rest of the train ride was pretty dry and boring. I plied them with dull, get-to-know-you questions. Enough to keep their minds off the fact they were about to do something absolutely stupid."

Olli made a thoughtful noise. "Sure. What about when you got here?"

Chapter 10
The One With The New City

A nthony half-swung, half-stepped off the last two steps of the train car and looked around the platform.

It was a beautiful terminal. It looked a lot like the terminal they had left in Bay City. Though this one, while still grand and in the modern style, was a bit more utilitarian. More blues, greens, and blacks here as well. Rather that the bright hues of Bay City.

Bay City was much more flashy and look-at-me. Bay City wanted the attention and the awe. New money.

Anthony liked this better.

Much more relaxed.

Calm.

Old money.

"Well. This is Big Town, huh?" Teo mused, stepping off the train car only a few minutes after him.

Eddy stepped off the step just a few seconds later and looked around quietly, adjusting his grip on the briefcase he was holding. "This is nice."

Anthony smiled at them and nodded. "Well. Perhaps I'll see you gents around sometime in the near future." He offered his hand to Teo.

Teo smiled brightly and shook his hand. "It was good to meet you, Anthony. Good luck on your ventures."

Anthony nodded and smiled a little before offering his hand to Eddy. "It was good talking to you, Eddy."

Eddy took his hand and shook it firmly. "You too, Anthony."

Anthony smiled and started to walk away from them. "Listen, you make that restaurant sale, and I see you two before you leave town. Dinner is on you two." He smirked and swung his finger between the two of them. "Eh? And it'll be a <u>good</u> one."

"You got it, friend." Teo laughed and shook his head a little. "Have a good day!"

Anthony smiled and walked away through the crowd.

"Wait!" Olli sat up straight sharply. "I don't understand. You just walked away from them?! How were you going to figure out where they were going?!"

Razor chuckled. "So impatient."

Olli shrugged a little, half shaking her head.

"If you gave me a couple more seconds..."

A slow smile pulled at Olli's lips. "You followed them."

"Of course I did." Razor smirked. "What did you take me for? An amateur?"

Olli snorted. "Sorry."

"You should be." Razor chuckled quietly and shifted his chair. "So. I walked away from them..."

Anthony walked through three large groups of people before pausing and looking back the way he had come from.

Teo and Eddy were standing near the train car, chatting with each other, clearly deciding what they were going to do.

Anthony stood where he was, ignoring the way that foot traffic moved around him. He watched them and waited to see what they would do. He was going to have to be careful now. At least until he caught where they were staying, they couldn't know he was following them anymore.

"Why not?" Olli protested.

Razor tilted his head slightly. "You're a clever girl. You tell me why you think I didn't want them to know I was following them."

Olli itched her scalp a little and made a thoughtful noise. "You wanted to see where they were staying...at this point had you decided if you were going to find Joey before <u>they</u> did?" She looked at him and raised an eyebrow.

Razor shook his head. "I hadn't honestly."

"So you wanted to kill time, see what the lay of the land was. Find a place that was close to them that you could keep tabs on them if you wanted. But far enough away they wouldn't be able to 'accidentally' run into you without you planning it first," Olli mused, almost to herself.

Razor smiled and nodded. "That's pretty much exactly what I was thinking."

Olli smiled a little and grunted. "Thank you. Where did they stay?"

"A little motel out of town." Razor wrinkled his nose a little in a disgusted sort of way. "Dirty little place." He shook his head a little. "It was just a few blocks from The Line."

Olli tilted her head a little and knit her eyebrows a little. "Why would they stay in a place like that? There's plenty of nice boarding houses between the train station and The District."

"Honestly, Doll, I'm not entirely sure they had the money to stay anywhere else. The trip over from Italy isn't a cheap one."

"What about you? You had money to stay someplace better, judging by that tone." Olli raised her eyebrows blandly.

Razor nodded. "About that..."

As soon as Teo and Eddy started to move toward the exit, Anthony walked after them, careful to not catch up to them too much. They weren't looking for him, but he didn't want to get them wondering either.

Neither seemed bright enough to see him for who he was. At least, not yet.

Anthony weaved through the crowd, lightly brushing against a few people as he walked.

"You picked pockets to get enough money to get you a nice place to stay..." Olli shook her head.

Razor shrugged slightly and smirked. "What did you expect me to do?"

"Certainly not get a job." Olli shook her head.

"I have a job." Razor shrugged.

Olli looked at him for a moment and scoffed. "Sure. We can call it that. How much money you scoop off those poor saps?"

Razor shrugged. "I'm really not sure, Doll. I doubt they even noticed it."

"You doubt they even noticed..." Olli half shook her head and laughed. "I know it was the twenties....but...Razor. People notice when money goes missing. Even when they're flush with cash."

Razor nodded and shrugged. "Care if I move this along? Or would you like to try to right a small wrong from the last decade?" He smirked a little, knowing he had trapped her.

Olli shook her head and leaned back into the chair again. "Go ahead."

Anthony walked out of the main station and looked around the new city he was standing in. A small smile crossed his face. It looked like most of the buildings were just a couple of decades old. Beautiful, tall, regal buildings.

Clearly, no cent held back.

But, as he looked around, he noticed the buildings to the West; the scene changed a bit. The buildings looked order, more utilitarian.

A little more run down.

Less loved.

Anthony wondered about that for a moment, trying to sort out why the building topography changed so much. On the other side of The Harbor, it seemed like all the life and money flowed from the water into the city.

Here it looked like the money went in the opposite direction...if at all.

Anthony glanced around and tried to pick out where Eddy and Teo had wandered off to. He couldn't lose them now.

<u>That</u> would be embarrassing.

He followed the two of them with nearly a half a block behind them. As he walked, Anthony glanced to see where they were in the crowd, but didn't lean enough to reveal himself if they happened to glance behind them.

Teo hailed a hack four blocks from the train station.

"Why did they walk <u>four blocks?!</u>" Olli tilted her head. "Wait...which direction from the station?"

Razor shrugged. "I don't know, Doll. Because they wanted to? It's not like I ran up and asked them to share a ride and tell me why they walked so far away since there was a line of hacks waiting to pick people up at the station."

Olli snorted. "Right. Sorry. They took that to the motel where you said they were staying?"

Razor nodded. "Went straight there and got a room."

Olli made a soft humming noise. "Where did you go next?"

Anthony looked out the window of the hack critically.

Of all the places in the world, someone would, or <u>could</u> go in a new city to hang their hat. This building was filthy. It didn't look like it had been used regularly in at least ten years.

"Wait! I think I know that place!" Olli suddenly sat up straighter. It's just a few blocks away from where the nice part of town starts to fade out. There's still a few people that live around there. I've heard a lot of hobos live in and around that hotel now." She pointed in the vague direction she was talking about.

Razor smirked and nodded a little. "You're not wrong. Are you all right if I just continue the story?"

Olli nodded. "Sorry. Just realized I knew where you were talking about."

Razor chuckled and shook his head. "It didn't look a whole lot better then. Maybe the paint was a bit more fresh. Either way..."

"You want me to bring you up to the main office?" the hackie in the front seat wondered, looking back at him.

Anthony shook his head a little. "No. No...actually, I was wondering if I could ask you something."

The hackie tilted his head and nodded a little. "Sure. What is it?"

"If you wanted to go somewhere....to have a good time. Where would you go?"

"Look, Mister—"

"Oh. I'm not law enforcement. I think your Prohibition laws are a waste of time and something to be worked around. Where would you go?"

The hackie shrugged a little and shook his head. "I wouldn't know. Sorry, friend."

Anthony shook his head a little and shrugged. "Not a problem. I'd like someplace to stay that isn't...whatever <u>that</u> is." He pointed at the motel across the street, a slight disgust crept into his tone.

"You got it buddy." The hackie smirked back at him slightly and pulled away from the curb he was parked next to. "Any place in particular you're hoping for?"

Anthony shook his head a little and smiled slightly. "No. Just not something that looks like no one has used it in the last ten years."

The hackie nodded once and started driving back toward town. "I think I know a place."

Chapter 11
The One With The Code Phrase

"Where'd you end up?" Olli tilted her head.

Razor made a thoughtful noise and stared into the middle-distance for a bit. "The little red and white boarding house on..." his voice trailed off a little as he thought. "Whats that little quiet street three blocks West of Ashland Street?"

Olli looked at him for a moment, her eyebrows half up. "Ashland Street?" she wondered, her tone completely boggled.

"Ashland Street." Razor repeated, nodding slightly.

"Saying it again doesn't..." Olli pursed her lips. "I don't know where Ashland Street is."

Razor stared at her for a moment. "You...don't."

Olli shook her head. "I've never seen it."

Razor stared at her for a moment and blinked a little. "You know where The Line is?"

"Obviously." Olli nodded.

"Five blocks East and three North." Razor gestured in the general direction he was explaining.

Olli's eyes followed his hand motion for a second. She made a thoughtful noise and pursed her lips together slightly. "Ashburry?"

Razor looked at her for a moment. "Ashburry?" He shook his head. "No. That doesn't sound right."

"The red and white boarding house? There's one on Ashburry. But it's...more pink now." Olli nodded.

Razor looked a little confused. "More pink?" he narrowed his eyes slightly.

"Yes." Olli nodded. "The red isn't all that red anymore cause it's been a while since it was painted."

"It has the large flowering tree in the spring?" Razor offered, his tone half unsure.

Olli nodded eagerly. "Yes! The tulip tree on Ashburry! With the little picket fence that's missing a few sections right by the house?"

Razor looked at her for a moment and processed the information. "Perhaps…"

Olli tilted her head and frowned. "It's right on the corner of Asburry. Where the three stop signs are?"

Razor grunted. He thought a bit more and then shrugged slightly. "I suppose it's not all that terribly important."

Olli shrugged and bobbed her head. "No. Guess not."

Anthony stepped out of the hack and reached back in to grab his suitcase, newspaper and fedora. "Thanks for the ride."

The hackie nodded and smiled with a slight wave. "Thanks for the tip."

Anthony nodded once and closed the back door. He knocked on the roof and stepped up onto the curb.

The hack pulled away from the curb and started back toward town.

Anthony watched for a moment before turning and walking to the little gate in the middle of the picket fence. He carefully opened the gate and walked into the garden. He looked up at the flowering tree on his left; all the flowers deep pink to white.

"You didn't have the hack wait while you checked to see if there was a room available?" Olli's eyebrow jumped up a couple of inches. "That doesn't seem very smart."

"I wasn't worried about it." Razor shrugged and smirked.

"Why not?" Olli tilted her head. "What would you do? Wander the streets and hope that you find a place with a bed?"

Razor chuckled. "No. I knew there was room."

Olli tilted an eyebrow at him. "You…knew…"

"Sure. There was a little sign that said there was vacancy." Razor smirked at her. "Right there, hanging over the mailbox."

Olli laughed a little and sighed. "Aces."

Razor chuckled. "So I booked my room, got settled in and spent some time trying to figure out how was going to find a party."

Olli nodded. "Ah yes. The most important thing when going to find Joey Leftfoot."

Razor nodded and tapped his nose. "Exactly."

Anthony walked down the front walk and swung the gate open. He stepped through, closed the gate behind him, and reached up to adjust his hat on his head. He looked both ways down the street and debated which direction he wanted to start.

Finding Joey Leftfoot was his primary focus at this point. Once he found him, that's when the inroads would start.

"About those inroads?" Olli held up her hand slightly.

Razor raised an eyebrow. "Yes?"

"What exactly was your plan? Since he _was_ gangster."

Razor shrugged a little. "At this point, I was thinking it would probably be best if I went with something a little less direct."

"Less direct..." Olli narrowed her eyes slightly and half turned her head, her tone clarifying. "Are you talking about...like what Teo and Eddy were talking about doing?"

Razor nodded. "I wasn't sure what I was going to sell him on at that point, but I _did_ know that people tend to want to buy things from people that they actually like."

"So...you planned to let him see you around for a while?" Olli assumed quietly.

Razor nodded. "Something like that."

"How long did it take you to find a party that Joey was actually throwing?" Olli smirked.

"Honestly, I think it was about three days later I finally tracked down someone willing to tell me what I wanted to know."

"It took you a whole three days?!" Olli laughed. "How long did it take Eddy and Teo to track him down?"

Razor smirked. "Longer, actually. _Much_ longer."

"How could you <u>possibly</u> know that?" Olli tilted her head slightly.

Razor shook his head. "You're getting ahead of me here, Doll."

"Oh. Aces. Sorry about that." Olli laughed quietly. "Go ahead. I'm listing."

Anthony walked through the front door of what looked like a bank. According to someone who told someone else; who told their friend's mother-in-law's second son's cousin's uncle, who told someone else; who told <u>him</u>...this was Big Town's <u>worst</u>, best kept secret.

This is where Joey Leftfoot hung his hat, apparently. Given one knew where to look for it.

And it only took him about two and a half days to find it.

Anthony walked down a hallway and smiled a little to himself when he heard the music start to gain volume.

He stepped up to the last door and knocked on it firmly.

While he waited for someone to open the door, he glanced back the way he had come from, checking to see he was the only one in the hallway.

A soft, sliding noise brought Anthony's attention back to the door in front of him.

"Good evening." Anthony smiled and pulled his fedora off his head.

"Who are you?" a gruff, distrusting voice wondered through the opening in the door.

"Ah. I was told to tell you that my name is Anthony, and that Larry sent me." He smiled at the man through the small slat.

The man on the other side was nothing more than an inch or so of forehead, a pair of distrustful brown eyes, and an inch or so of a flat-bridged nose.

Nothing happened for a moment before the slat snapped shut.

Anthony stood where he was, holding his fedora in his hand, the other hand pushed loosely into his pocket. He had expected the reaction, and now it was just waiting for the code word to be trusted. He lightly tapped the bottom of the brim of his hat against his thigh while he waited.

Just when Anthony started to wonder if he was going to be locked out forever, the door opened.

"Welcome to the party." The man behind the door opened it and gestured for Anthony to come inside.

Anthony smiled at him in a charming way and stepped through the door. "Thank you." He smirked at the man with the flat-bridged nose. "You waited just long enough for me to start to worry. You must be paid well."

The flat-bridged nose man grunted and shut the door with a quiet push.

Anthony smiled and pointed toward the rest of the room. He walked away from the door, lightly dropping his fedora back on his head. As he walked into the main room, Anthony paused to look around for a moment.

Olli cleared her throat. "It looked like a bank?" She wondered, her tone thoughtful.

Razor nodded. "The building isn't there anymore. But it said..." Razor paused for a moment, looking thoughtful. "County Bank and Trust over the front door. I walked through the side door."

Olli looked at him for a moment. "Right through the side door? Just like that."

Razor nodded. "It was the '20s, Doll. They weren't exactly hiding it once you knew who to ask."

Olli looked at him for a moment, processing what he had said. "Was Joey at that party?" she wondered, deciding not to ask any more questions.

Razor shook his head. "No."

"No?" Olli looked at him for a minute, her tone and look completely puzzled. "But..."

"It was part of the plan." Razor assured.

Olli tilted her head a little. "It...was?"

Razor nodded. "Think about it, Doll," he coaxed.

Olli sat quietly for a moment. "Explain." She rested her temple against the knuckles of her right fist as she set her elbow on the arm on the chair.

"I didn't want to just waltz in and introduce myself to him."

"No. Why would you want to be that direct?" Olli tilted her head, sarcasm deep in her tone. "You might save yourself some time."

Razor chuckled. "But, Doll. Remember the reason I was there in the first place. I wanted to sell him on something. It's hard to do that when you just walked through the door. Cold selling a mafia don is a large undertaking. And I figured I had more than enough time to try for the warm sell. And in order to do that, the first thing I wanted to do was get people used to seeing me around the clubs. Makes me appear more trustworthy."

Olli laughed a little. "Boy...Joey must have been <u>so</u> surprised when you conned him."

Razor shrugged. "It ended up working in my favor."

"How many parties did you have to go to before you finally crossed paths with Joey?" Olli wondered, adjusting how she was sitting a little.

"Larry sent me to four parties."

"<u>Four</u>?!"

Chapter 12
The One With The Ex-Boxer

"Sure. Four parties." Razor shrugged and smiled. "I wanted him to get used to seeing me around. Hear about me. Not see me as a threat."

Olli took a breath and nodded a little. "Sure. That makes sense, I suppose."

Razor shrugged a bit. "By the time I arrived at the fifth party, I met the man himself."

"Joey talked to you?"

Razor nodded. "In passing."

Anthony sat on a simple wooden stool and leaned one elbow on the bar top. He sipped his drink and looked around the inside of this building.

He hadn't been to this one before.

It was a nice building.

And clearly the clientele here had a lot more money to throw around than at the last four parties.

Jewels dripped off the ladies, and even a few men. There were feathers, headdresses, beautiful watches, impressive cigars. Backless dresses waltzed by in every color imaginable, fringe and wide-swinging skirts bouncing wildly.

Anthony liked this place.

It felt like it was the sort of place a mob boss would hang out. He turned on the stool and looked back toward the door when it seemed like there was some to-do going on there.

The bouncers shooed people away from the door. The man closest to the door opened it wide and invited the person on the other side in with a large sweeping gesture of his arm.

Anthony sipped his drink and watched the people walk into the room one after the other. There were about ten of them.

It was unusual that many people were coming in all at the same time. The most that had walked through the door at one time at the last four parties he was at were usually two couples.

Ten was...interesting.

"That <u>had</u> to be Joey and his posse," Olli mused in a tone that was more to herself than anything. "I heard he always traveled in a pack."

Razor grunted and nodded. "I'm aware."

Olli focused on him and scoffed a little. "That's right. You used to travel <u>in</u> that posse."

Razor nodded and smiled a little. "That I did. Just off his right shoulder."

Olli made a thoughtful noise. "Were you assigned that spot? Or did you just end up there?"

Razor looked thoughtful for a moment, and shrugged a little. "I'm sorry, Doll. I really don't remember."

Olli bobbed her head and half shrugged. "It's all right. I suppose it's not all that important." She sucked her teeth for a moment. "There were nine people with him? That's a lot of bodyguards."

Razor shook his head a little and smirked. "Two of them were a little too pretty to be gangsters."

Olli puzzled for a moment before nodding slowly. "Right. Pretty girls. Of course."

The girls could have been more than twenty. One a fancy brunette in a wine-red dress with enough black fringe to almost cover her pale legs to her knees. Stark white gloves ran all the way up to her elbows. Flashy jewels dripped from her ears and draped around her neck, matching the rings on nearly every finger and the bangles on her arms.

A platinum blonde flounced next to her, hugging her left arm tightly. She wore a bright green dress with silver brocade overlays. Her hair was bobbed short and straight, almost to her ears. Bright-red lip stain, and shockingly-blue eye shadow. She didn't have gloves, but she was draped in just as much finery as her counterpart.

Both girls' lashes were nearly three times the size they should have been.

"Was that Birdie?" Olli piped up, sitting up straight and looking at him sharply.

"If you're referring to the girl that sings for me on occasion—"

"Because every night is an occasion..." Olli intoned in a dull tone, one eyebrow half moving up fractionally.

"Then no. She was too young to be hanging on Joey's arm back then."

"That doesn't mean she wasn't." Olli pointed out. You know that as well as I do."

Razor chuckled. "She tended to be on _my_ arm than any other."

Olli leaned back into the left corner of the wing-backed chair she was sitting in. "Sure. That makes sense."

Razor's eyebrow went up fractionally. "What...what was that tone, exactly?"

Olli smirked and shook her head a little. "Don't worry about it. So there were two girls. _Clearly,_ they amused you. What about the guys with them?"

Razor shrugged. "The usual suspects. _He_ was there—"

"Two-Timer?" Olli assumed.

Razor grunted. "I never understood why Joey took him places. He may have been the manager of the clubs, but he always looked like death warmed over and..." his voice trailed off while his face scrunched up slightly. "_Slippery._"

Olli snorted. "I've seen him. Once or twice."

Anthony pulled his gaze away from the two girls, interested to see who would come in with such a large group and have a pair of angels with him.

There were a couple of intimidating looking bruisers in the pack, scanning the place. Clearly, they were looking for a threat.

There were a few other men with them. All various ages, dressed like they had more money than they knew what to do with.

One of them was at the older edge of the scale, pale features, with almost a greyish hue to them. He had salt and pepper hair cropped short. He looked around critically, almost like a manager would after being away from the business for a bit. Like he wanted to make sure everything was running as he instructed it to be when he returned.

But the one that Anthony focused on for the longest was the plain-looking man that walked near the middle of the group. Unlike the others, he seemed more self-possessed.

He walked like he owned the place. Just like his build, his hair was an average brown color, flecks of grey spattered around his ears and the top of his head.

Joey Leftfoot.

There were two things about his appearance that gave Anthony pause, convincing him that <u>this</u> was the man he was looking for.

The first was the nose on his face—Roman and probably substantial at one point, now flattened and broken a few too many times into a half-mangled mess. The tip of it kicked to the left, there was a harsh bulge on the right edge, halfway to his eyes. The ridge between his eyes was flattened sharply.

Boxing injuries, most likely. They made sense with the healed-over scars on his cheekbones and on his jaw.

He may have looked plain and unlikely. But a second look at his face hinted the man was more dangerous than a cursory glance made it seem.

"I read somewhere once that he got his nickname in the boxing ring," Olli mused quietly. "He was one of the last bare-knuckle fighters in this area."

Razor grunted and nodded. "He used to tell stories about it when he was feeling especially...fond of the past."

Olli made a thoughtful noise. "You said there were two things?"

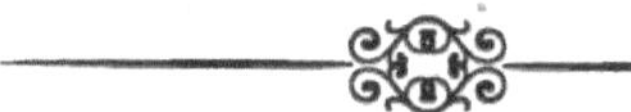

His eyes were the main reason Anthony was sure this was who he was looking for. They were hard. Almost reptilian. They scanned the world around, looking at any and all people like they were a threat...or a purse.

Anthony smiled to himself.

The ex-boxer was his target.

Joey Leftfoot looked around the room again, his eyes running over the bar until they reached Anthony.

A slight look of recognition crossed his face.

Chapter 13
The One With The Plan Coming Together

Olli looked at him and flared her eyes slightly and bit her lip excitedly. "He recognized you!"

Razor nodded. "I hadn't seen him at the last couple of parties. But...I hadn't really been looking for him either. I wanted to be seen, but not be up front about it."

Olli laughed a little and shook her head a bit. "Aces. You tell a good story. I'm excited and I wasn't even there."

Razor chuckled. "I love it when a plan comes together. You share that feeling with me."

Olli smirked for a moment before she cleared her throat and looked at him with a stiff, stern look. "We're not supposed to be friends."

Razor chuckled, and he shook his head a little. "I won't tell if you don't."

Olli stared at him for a moment and slowly shook her head. "Just tell the story."

Razor chuckled a little more and looked pleased with himself. "All right."

Anthony sipped his drink and smiled a little over the rim when he made eye contact. In a distant, friendly way.

Much like you would to a stranger on a train.

Or someone you passed on the sidewalk.

Joey Leftfoot was no fool. He was not the type to be reeled in by warm, friendly smile and overtly personal passes.

Better to let the big game come to <u>him</u>.

Joey looked at him for a minute, no reaction on his face. One eyebrow went up fractionally before he turned and caught the attention of the two girls walking with him. Leading them toward the large circular booth, the gorillas had scoped out for him.

Anthony stayed put, sipping his drink, chatting with people who wandered up to the bar, even half-making friends with the man behind the bar pouring.

This sort of thing was what Joey would notice over time. Someone new, but who fit into the world he had created for himself.

Anthony's one goal was to set things up so Joey would see him as someone who would and <u>should</u> be part of his world. Someone he could trust to spend his time with. It wasn't something that could be rushed. It was something that required the utmost patience.

If the plan came together the way that he wanted and needed it to, he was going to have to play the long game for a while. Spend a bit more money. Get on a face basis with as many bartenders as he could.

First-name would be even better.

The more people from Joey's life that knew who he was and felt comfortable with him, the more likely Joey wouldn't think twice about entertaining a conversation or two with him. Even if they were short conversations.

Small steps were what mattered.

Olli sighed in a soft, impatient way. She looked at him and raised an eyebrow when he gave her an unimpressed look. "I get it. You wanted him to see you as completely unimposing and <u>totally</u> non-threatening. Like the innocent schoolboy you are." She smirked at him.

Razor snorted. "Something like that."

"All right. So. Tell me how long it took for you to actually interact with him that night." Olli shifted, picking up her left foot and hooking it under her right knee.

"Oh, I didn't. Not really."

Olli's left eyebrow dipped sharply. "What?"

Razor tilted his head a little. "Why don't you just let me tell the story in order?"

Olli folded her arms. "Normally that wouldn't be a problem, but you tell stories like Monet painted! One little impressionist dot at a time."

Razor looked at her and sat up a little straighter. He smirked a little and looked incredibly proud. "You know who Monet is!" he clapped his hands a little and grinned at her. "How incredibly wonderful!"

Olli stared at him for a moment. "Razor...I went to school. I've been to a museum or two."

"On purpose?"

Olli's mouth popped open before snapping shut with some finality. "There's no need to be rude. I'm told I come from high breeding. Which means I know about the finer things in life."

Razor didn't have the decency to look chided. "I have never been so proud of you."

Olli stared at him for a moment. "How long was Joey there that night?"

"What night?"

"The night. The one you're talking about. With the gorillas and the girls!" Olli looked at him in a half-exasperated way.

Razor chuckled and shrugged a little. "The whole night."

"Get you another one, Mack?" the bartender paused in front of Anthony and smiled a little, using a simple, white towel to shine up a pint glass.

"Anthony." Anthony smiled and pointed at himself with his right first finger.

"Anthony. Nice to meet you. Get cha another?" the bartender repeated, his tone not bored, but not all that committed to the introduction.

Anthony looked at his glass for a moment and made a thoughtful noise. "How many is this?" he wondered, setting his finger on the rim of the glass in front of him.

"Two." The bartender shrugged a little.

Anthony thought for a moment, mentally counting through the money in his pocket. He nodded and smiled in a bright charming way. "Sure. I'll have another...?" he paused, waiting for a name from the man behind the bar.

"Charley."

"I'll have another one, please, Charley." Anthony smiled warmly.

Charley smiled a little and nodded. "You got it..." he smiled at him. "Anthony." He hustled away, looking at another patron that walked up to the bar.

Anthony watched after him, and sipped at his drink. He turned around on the stool slightly, leaning one elbow on the bar top, watching the band play for a bit. A smile crossed his face. They were cracking along with a bright tune, drawing couples out onto the dance floor, pulling them from the tables and booths that surrounded it.

His eyes wandered to the booth where one large man leaned on the wall, and the other stood half a couple of feet away, between the rest of the room and the booth. Both seemed to be having a good time.

Watchful, but a good time.

Anthony leaned his back against the edge of the bar and smiled a bit at a couple of people that passed him. He swirled the liquid in his drink a little and watched people move around the bar.

There were some that he recognized.

They had been at one or more of the parties he had been. A couple of them even recognized him. One or two wandered over and said hello, chatting for a bit.

After a bit and the stream of people walking up to the bar slowed down, Anthony turned to lean on it again, chatting with Charley when the bartender had a few minutes.

It had been almost forty minutes when Anthony felt like someone was next to him. He looked over in a half curious way.

"Hi there. Have I seen you around here before?"

Chapter 14
The One With The Slow and Steady Approach

"That's the first thing that he said to you?" Olli tilted her head a little, looking slightly disappointed. "That was... anticlimactic."

Razor chuckled and shrugged a little. "I'm not sure what you were expecting."

"Something...<u>better</u> than that." Olli wrinkled her nose. "I was hoping for something more...." her hands waved around a little while she searched for the word.

"What? Like something fitting for a mob boss?" Razor wondered, one eyebrow going up.

"Aces...when you say it like that, it sounds so stupid." Olli rolled her eyes and looked at him wryly.

Razor shrugged a little and puffed on his cigar. "Sorry, Doll."

Olli scoffed slightly. "So. The big man himself walked up and said hello. Just like that?"

Razor nodded. "Just like that."

"Why?"

"I really don't know." Razor shrugged. "Honestly, I wasn't watching. I had just been chatting with Charley."

Olli bobbed her head a little, like the answer made sense. "All right then. What happened next?"

"...Hi there. Have I seen you around here before?"

Anthony looked over his right arm and blinked in surprise. "No." He shook his head a little. "Not here. You might have seen me around at a couple of other parties here and there."

Joey Leftfoot looked at him and nodded a little. "Have another, Charley?" he wondered, not looking away from Anthony while he said it.

"You got it, Boss." Charley's voice agreed like he was walking past.

"One for my new friend too, will ya?" Joey's voice drifted over his shoulder as Charley walked away, though he didn't turn from looking over Anthony. His gaze cold and predatorial, waiting for Anthony to flinch under his gaze.

Charley paused and glanced back. He nodded and kept walking.

Anthony smiled slightly and nodded once. "That's very generous of you." He lounged against the bar, not bothering to move, and not flinching under the gaze that Joey looked over him with.

Joey shrugged. "We're all here to have a good time. You have a good time, you spend more money at my little get togethers. Win-win for the both of us, wouldn't you say?" Joey smirked quietly for a moment. "Seems to me that's well worth the price of a single drink. Do you?"

"You're the boss." Anthony smirked.

Joey smirked and grunted. "I suppose that's what they say."

Charley walked past and dropped off a glass next to both of them on his way past to take the orders from a couple of new patrons that had walked up behind Anthony.

Anthony picked up the glass and half hefted it to him in a silent thank you. "To the party."

Joey picked up his glass and clinked it against Anthony's. "To the party."

Olli bit her lips together and half stifled a giggle.

Razor raised an eyebrow. "Yes?"

"You did that on purpose," Olli smirked at him and tilted her head a little as one eyebrow moved up fractionally.

"Not <u>everything</u> that I do and say is on <u>purpose</u>." Razor shook his head and looked at her seriously for a minute.

Olli looked at him for a moment and shook her head. "Sure." She shook her head a little. "I can see you smirking. But sure."

"However...that particular time it was on purpose." Razor proudly and puffed on his cigar.

"Instant way to stroke his ego and make him feel like he was superior to you?" Olli wondered, tilting her head slightly, her tone thoughtful.

Razor tapped the side of his nose and pulled the cigar from between his lips to gently blow the smoke up toward the ceiling.

"Clever." Olli smiled a little.

Razor made a noise like he had expected her to say as much.

Joey looked at him for a moment and smiled like a shark. "What's your name, friend?" He glanced around the room, surveilling the party in a calm, almost proud way. He looked back and took a sip of his drink, looking expectant.

"Anthony."

"You told <u>him</u> your real name right off the bat like that?!" Olli's voice cracked.

Razor looked at her like he had expected more from her. "We're not talking about some no-name, terrible con man team that wouldn't know a real name from a <u>fake</u>." He clicked his tongue and shook his head a little. "Come on now. This is Joey Leftfoot we're talking about here. The man had connections back to Italy. I may have been from a small town in the middle of nowhere, but if Joey wanted to find out who I was. He would have."

Olli nodded and looked a little chastised. She blinked suddenly and looked up at him. "He <u>did</u> didn't he?"

"Did what?"

"He checked up on you!" Olli smirked at him, tilting her head slightly.

Razor shrugged. "I'm really not sure. Not <u>sure</u> sure. If you know what I mean."

Olli smirked at him and nodded. "But you suspect."

Razor dipped his chin. "I do. And I did." He bounced his shoulders a little. "Figured, either way, if Teo and Eddy showed up and used the name that I gave them—"

"Your real name."

"Yes. My real name. Joey wouldn't suddenly have a reason to find a creative way to make me...disappear."

Olli grunted slightly and bobbed her head. "That makes sense."

"Cons really only work if you're around to collect the money at the end of them." Razor smirked.

Olli snorted. "What happened next?"

"What's your name, friend?" glanced around the room, surveilling the party in a calm, almost proud way. He looked back and took a sip of his drink, looking expectant.

"Anthony."

Joey smiled at him a little and sipped his drink again. "Well. <u>Anthony</u>. It's good to meet you. You should come around more often."

Anthony nodded and sipped his drink. "Thank you. I think I will."

"I'll drink to that." Joey smiled a little, picked up his glass and clinked the bottom of his glass against the top few inches of Anthony's new glass. "Enjoy the party." The shark smile flashed one more time as Joey stood up straight and walked away from the bar.

Anthony half turned and watched him go for a moment.

"You really caught his attention, Mack." Charley mused, looking over at him, polishing an ever-present glass again. "He rarely buys people drinks."

Anthony inspected the glass that Joey had pushed toward him. "Is that so?"

"And an invite from the Boss means you get in without a fuss, no matter what." Charley nodded and smirked at him a little.

Anthony made a thoughtful noise and bobbed his head slightly. "Haven't had much fuss so far. Good to know that isn't going to start up soon." He smirked and took another sip of his drink.

Charley held the glass up and inspected the job he had done against the shine of the lights overhead. "Looks like it's shaping up to be a great night."

Anthony nodded and smiled a little. "That it does."

"Did you go over and talk to him after that?" Olli wondered, tilting her head.

Razor shook his head. "No. I didn't."

"Why not? He had basically invited you over." Olli frowned slightly.

"You're trying to rush it." Razor shook his head. "Slow and steady wins the race."

"Aesop's Fable."

"It applies to working a mark just as well as it does to a normal world situation. Push the mark too fast and you're all set up to ruin the plan before it even gets started. Let the mark come to you..." He shrugged and winked at her. "That's when the magic happens. You can't rush perfection."

Olli nodded a little. "What did you do next?"

Razor's right shoulder twitched a little, and he puffed his cigar. "I stayed where I was. Chatted with Charley more when he had the time between other people coming up to the bar...drank a bit more. Talked to people who happened to wander over and sit near me."

Olli nodded a little. "Basically just...being seen but not pitching an idea."

Razor nodded and tapped his nose before picking up his glass and sipping from it. "Exactly."

"Because slow and steady." Olli raised an eyebrow at him.

"Slow and Steady."

Chapter 15
The One With The Card Game

"All right. I think we've spent enough time on slow and steady for this part of the story." Olli smirked at him. "Skip to an exciting part."

"Are you telling me that you're not having a good time?" Razor wondered, raising his eyebrow slightly.

Olli shrugged slightly. "I'm just saying that you don't have to draw this out for my benefit."

Razor chuckled softly and bobbed his head. He puffed his cigar and looked thoughtful for a moment. "Any particular place where you would like me to jump to?"

Olli shook her head. "Not really."

Razor made a thoughtful noise. "All right. I think I can handle that."

The next few nights Anthony went to every party that he was invited to, dancing and drinking the nights away.

"Wait!" Olli held up a hand. "I have a question."

Razor made a noise in the back of his throat and looked at her like he was expecting the interruption. "Yes?"

"What about the money? I never went, but I hear those parties sucked up a <u>lot</u> of money for Joey."

Razor chuckled. "That they did."

"You weren't running a con, and it sounds like you burned through all of your money getting here." Olli tilted her head. "You even played pick pocket in the train station!"

Razor scoffed. He chuckled and shook his head. "I just did that for <u>fun</u>. A little walking around money."

Olli looked at him and arched an eyebrow.

Razor sighed and nodded once. "All right. I was a bit strapped for cash, and I didn't want to pilfer pockets at the parties—"

"Bad form to rob the people you're about to rob," Olli agreed, cutting him off.

Razor chuckled and nodded a little. "Exactly."

"So? What did you do for walking around money?" Olli tilted her head.

"I brought my favorite party trick." Razor smirked.

"Hey. Back up. Give the man some room to at least sit down before you all crowd him! Can't play the game if he can't!" Charley ordered, shooing people back with his hands and the towel he almost always had over his shoulder. "Go on! Let him breathe, will ya?"

"It's all right, Charley," Anthony assured, waving him off. "Really. The people are just excited." He pulled a chair out and dropped into it loosely. He shifted the chair closer to the table and unbuttoned the button on his suit coat. Once he was ready, Anthony reached into the inner pocket and pulled out three cards.

The large group of people pushed in around him excitedly. Everyone was holding drinks in their hands and smiling brightly.

Anthony smiled at them and gestured to the only other chair directly across from him at the table. "All right. Who's feeling lucky today? Take a seat—thank you Charley." He smiled as a glass was set next to him by the ever-attentive Charley.

Charley nodded and patted his shoulder before walking back to the bar.

Anthony shuffled the three cards in his hands and waited for someone to sit down across from him. "Come on! Don't be shy!

It's just a game!" He gestured to the empty chair. "Don't leave me hanging here, folks. Let's play the game!"

A girl in a bright cream, sparkly dress dropped into the chair with a giggle. "I'll play!" She grinned.

Anthony smiled at her and took a sip of his drink. "Well, wonderful!" He shuffled the cards and smiled at her softly. "All right. We all know the rules of the game?" His eyes ran around the group and settled on her. "Well, I saw a couple of nods, and more faces that I don't recognize, so I'll just run over them again. The game is Find The Lady." Anthony looked around the group dramatically. "In my hand you see I have three cards-" He held up the cards and showed them—face forward—to the crowd and the girl in the cream dress with a smirk. "You'll notice that there's only one queen. Much like you-" he winked at the girl across from him.

She tittered and covered her mouth slightly with her hand. She smiled brightly at him and nodded.

"Now. The game is simple, really. I'm going to lay the cards on the table and shuffle them up so neither of us know where the lady is. And _that's_ where you come in." He smiled at the girl across from him again brightly. "It's a pay to play, but don't worry—it's just a dollar—and that's nothing after everything you've spent so far." He smiled and set the cards face down on the table. "Now. If you find the lady—"—he pointed at the girl across from him with a smile—"I'll pay you three dollars. If you don't...well...I keep the dollar."

The girl nodded eagerly and smiled at him. "I'm ready," she tittered again. She pulled out a clutch purse that matched her dress and clicked the clasp open. After a minute of digging, she pulled out a single dollar and set it on the table. Her smile was large and bright.

Anthony smiled and spaced the three cards out in front of him. Once he was happy with the spacing, he fished into the pocket of his waistcoat and pulled out a small wad of cash. He unfolded it and peeled off three dollar bills. He set them down on the table near him and put the rest of the money back into the pocket in his waistcoat. "All right. Let's get this show on the road, shall we?" He smiled at her and started to flip the cards over so the faces were up. "Oh and, folks—"—he looked around him at the crowd—"side bets are not only all right, but they _are_ encouraged."

The crowd chuckled a little.

Anthony smiled and flipped the last card over. "There she is!" he tapped the queen card and smiled at the girl across from him. "You ready, Dish?"

The girl giggled and nodded brightly, biting her lip. "Yes!" she clapped her hands and grinned at the crowd and then at Anthony before turning her attention to the cards between them.

Anthony smiled at her. "All right. Keep an eye on her majesty, everyone." Anthony started to flip the cards back over. "And the card too." He winked at the girl across the table.

The girl blushed and giggled again.

A small chuckle rippled through the crowd.

Anthony smiled and started to move the cards around. "All right, all right. Keep an eye on her. Don't let her get away!" He moved the cards around, over, and down on themselves. He glanced up at the girl and smiled. "You just tell me when you want me to stop, Dish."

The girl bit her lip, looking at the cards closely. "Stop!" she called a couple of seconds later.

Anthony stopped and pulled his hands back from the cards. He laid them on the table and smiled. "All right, babydoll. You tell me. Think you can find the lady?"

The girl gnawed her lip for a moment and pointed at the middle card. "That one."

Anthony reached forward, but instead of flipping over the card she had pointed at, he tipped over the far-right card.

It was the ten of hearts.

The whole crowd seemed to lean in a bit.

Anthony smirked at her. "Now...what do you think? Do you want to double down on that answer? Or do you want to change the card for the money you're in now?" He looked at her and raised his eyebrow slightly.

"So <u>that's</u> how you made your money!" Olli laughed a little. "You coaxed gamblers into gambling more." She laughed again and scoffed.

Razor shrugged and smirked. "Of course I did!"

"But if she had doubled down, and she won?" Olli shrugged a little and tilted her head.

"She still made a dollar. You'd be amazed how thrilled people are with making a dollar." Razor smiled. "Plus, it strokes their ego and makes them feel like they're brighter than me."

Olli shook her head slightly and clicked her tongue.

Razor smirked and leaned back into his chair deeply. "It's all right. You can say it."

Olli looked at him and pulled her head back a little. "Say what?"

"You think I'm clever."

Olli snorted. "Did she find the lady?"

"You changing the subject doesn't change the fact that you think it." Razor smiled at her.

The girl thought for a moment and set another bill on the table on top of the one already there. "She's there," she announced.

Razor looked at her for a moment like he was nervous and didn't know how he was going to take her money. "All right. Here we go..." he reached for the middle card and smiled at her tightly.

The crowd leaned forward, straining to see the card.

Anthony flipped the middle card over so it was right side up.

The queen of hearts showed.

"Congratulations!" Anthony grinned through the cheers of the crowd around them. "You've found the lady!"

Chapter 16
The One With The Fishing

The girl gasp-squealed and both of her hands rushed up to her mouth. She giggled wildly before pulling her hands away and clapping them together wildly. Her lips were pulled back as far as she could get them in a large grin.

Anthony chuckled and scooped up the three bills on his side of the table and offered them to her. "All right. To the victor, the spoils. Well <u>done,</u> it's a hard game!"

The girl took them and set them on the pile of bills she had personally laid down. She giggled and clapped her hands. "I want to play again." She looked at him brightly.

"You did that on purpose!" Olli laughed.

"Of course I did!" Razor agreed. "The first few are always a gimme." He smirked. "<u>Especially</u> if the one playing is a pretty girl."

Olli shook her head. "Easier to draw people in that way?"

Razor nodded. "Exactly. You make the game too hard, people won't play. And that defeats the whole point."

Olli snorted and shook her head slightly. "I guess that makes sense."

"And when people are winning enough that people are drawn to it, then you can start to make some real money."

"Wait...did Joey know you were scamming people out of money at his parties?" Olli sat up a little straighter.

Razor looked indignant for a moment. "<u>Scamming</u>?!" he protested. "Olli, <u>really!</u>"

"Oh, I'm sorry. What would <u>you</u> call it?"

"I told you. It's a party trick."

Olli tilted her head a little and one eyebrow went up. "But you took their money."

"That they <u>willingly</u> gave to me," Razor pointed out.

"Fine. <u>Aces,</u> fine..." Olli held up her hands. "Did Joey know that you were party tricking people at his parties into paying for you to be there?"

Razor looked at her for a moment and laughed brightly. "Party tricking! That's fantastic! Do you mind if I use that?"

Olli shrugged a little and shook her head. "No. Not at all." She shot him a look like she really wasn't sure why he was asking her permission for such an off-the-wall thing.

Razor grinned at her and sipped his drink. "And to answer your question, yes. He did."

"And he didn't do anything about it?"

Razor hemmed and hawed for a moment. "I wouldn't go <u>that</u> far."

"How far <u>would</u> you go?" Olli wondered, one eyebrow going up slightly.

"It was the reason that I had an <u>actual</u> conversation with him." Razor smirked.

"Aces <u>finally</u>!" Olli threw her hands up in the air and shook her head slightly. "I was starting to wonder if we were <u>ever</u> going to get there."

"And not in the way that you think." Razor smirked.

Olli smirked. "Oh. I am very careful not to assume with you."

"And that is what makes you such a good detective." Razor smiled at her.

"All right. Surprise me." Olli's eyebrow went up slightly and looked at him like she was almost daring him to shock her.

Anthony groaned with the rest of the crowd around him as he flipped over the card that had been chosen. "Oh! You were having such a <u>great</u> run!"

The man across from him groaned and rubbed his face for a moment and shook his head. He sighed and shook his head, but pushed the small pile of money toward Anthony. "Good game though."

Anthony leaned forward and nodded a little. "It was." He gathered up the money and started to sort it into a neater pile.

The man across from him shrugged, gave him a good-natured smile, and stood up out of the chair.

"Thanks for playing." Anthony smiled at him. "I appreciate it."

The man nodded and melted into the crowd.

Anthony sipped his drink as he pushed the money into the inner pocket of his suit coat. "Have a nice night, thanks so much for playing." He glanced around the group slightly. "All right. Who wants to play next?" He wondered.

"I think I would."

The group around the table split like the school of fish around a shark, as the man who spoke stepped forward and walked to the table, closing ranks behind him as soon as he had passed.

Joey Leftfoot himself stepped up to the chair that was empty now. He pulled it out slightly for himself and dropped into it like a big cat, smiled at Anthony across the table. He sipped from the glass he was holding slowly. Joey slowly set the glass down on the table and tapped his fingertips on the top edge of the glass lightly. "If that's all right with you, Anthony."

Anthony carefully pulled his hand out of his suit coat and looked over at him for a moment. "Of course. Why would I say no?"

Joey smirked and chuckled. "That's the right answer, Anthony." He picked up his glass and sipped from it again.

Olli stared at Razor for a moment, something like controlled terror on her face. "That <u>had</u> to be unnerving."

Razor tilted his head a little. "I'm not sure what you mean."

"Joey Leftfoot. Just sitting down in front of you demanding to play like that?"

Razor chuckled quietly and smirked. "Honestly. I'm surprised it took him as long as it did to come over to play. It was the fifth party that I had that table and we played find the lady. And by the time he sat down <u>that</u> night...I'd been at it for almost two hours."

Olli looked at him for a moment, understanding dawning over her face. "You were <u>fishing</u>."

Razor made a noise of agreement. "I was."

"What happened next?" Olli leaned forward on her elbows, bracing them on the top of her thighs.

Anthony shuffled the cards and smirked a little. "Would you like a practice round, Boss?"

Joey looked at him for a moment, his head tilted. He looked at Anthony for a bit, his face completely devoid of emotion for almost an entire minute. Just when the silence stretched a little too long, a slow smirk started to pull at his lips. "You give anyone else a practice round, Anthony?"

"No, Boss." Anthony shook his head. "But they get the rundown about the rules before they play."

"Assume I know how to play." Joey looked at him steadily, smirked, and picked up his glass to take a small sip from it.

Anthony nodded once and set the three cards out on the table. "Sure, Boss."

Joey unbuttoned his suit coat and reached into it. He pulled out a pair of bills and set them on the table. "Play the game, Anthony." He put the bills on the table, sipped his drink slowly and set the glass down on the money.

Anthony glanced at the bills and nodded. He flipped the cards over and started to move the cards around. "Now. Remember. The point of the game is to find the lady. You find her, I pay you six dollars. You don't find her. I get the money on the table."

Joey watched the cards for a moment before looking up at Anthony. "I think that's enough, Anthony."

Anthony stopped moving the cards around and held his hands up and off the cards, waiting for Joey to pick the card he wanted.

Joey waited a bit. He sipped his drink slowly and set the glass back down on the small stack of bills before looking at Anthony. "Far right."

Anthony looked at him and flipped the card that was furthest right.

The entire group gasped and clapped when the queen of hearts appeared.

"Ah! Look at that! You found the lady!" Anthony praised. He smiled and dug into his pocket. He pulled out a pile of bills from his pocket and counted off a couple of bills, offering them to Joey across the table. "Your six dollars, Boss."

The shark grin was back. "Thank you, Anthony." Joey took the money and set it on top of the bills he had set on the table. He sat where he was for a moment before sipping his drink. "Good game." he stood up, swiped the money off the table and pushed it into his suit pocket. He looked at Anthony for a long moment, sipped his drink and nodded once, before stepping toward the crowd.

The people split in front of him like a well-oiled machine, giving way around him and closing rank behind him again.

A school of fish, split by an apex predator.

Chapter 17
The One With The Nickname

Anthony sat in the same position he had been sitting when Joey stood up, watching him leave. He blinked once the group had closed ranks and put on a bright smile when his newest victim sat down and pulled out a bill. "Ready to play the game?" he wondered, shuffling the cards.

The man nodded and watched the cards.

"What was the plan?" Olli wondered, lounging sideways in the chair. She had her back against one arm of the chair and her knees hooked over the other arm.

Razor tilted his head a little. "I'm not sure I understand."

Olli folded her arms loosely over her torso. "Even now, you look proud of yourself. Like there's something that you're hiding, just waiting for the big reveal."

"When? Then or now?" Razor's eyebrows jumped up fractionally as he sipped from his glass.

"Both." Olli shrugged.

"If I just <u>tell</u> you the plan, it loses all its..." he floundered for a word, his hand swirling around, trying to bring the word to his mind.

"Takes away all the drama?" Olli offered, smirking slightly.

"Well...yes." Razor didn't look satisfied with the word Olli had chosen, but was willing to accept it.

Olli snorted. "All right. Go ahead. What happened after that game ended for the night?"

"Right. The game ended...maybe four hours later."

"Aces! Four hours later?!" Olli scoffed. "You played that game for six hours!?"

Razor shrugged a little. "Five...six hours. I don't really remember."

"That's a long time to play a game." Olli hooked her ankles together and swung them a little. "Sounds like you made a lot of money."

Razor's right shoulder twitched. "I did all right."

"Nice hedge." Olli smirked. "What happened when the game broke up?"

Anthony smiled around at the crowd as he gathered up the three cards and pushed them together into a neat pile. "I think that's about it, everyone." He set the cards in the pocket of his waistcoat. "Thank you so much for playing! We'll try again next time."

The crowd started to disperse. Some of them patted his shoulder or grinned at him before walking away. About half wandered toward the dance floor, a lively tune had just started and they had decided to strap on their dancing shoes. The other half wandered toward the bar, hoping Charley could help them wet their whistles.

"Boss wants to talk to you." a voice informed, a step and a half behind Anthony's left shoulder.

Anthony blinked and continued to look over the group leaving in front of him. One eyebrow went up fractionally. He nodded once and stood up as he placed the three cards into the inner pocket of his jacket. "I'm assuming that he means right now?" he wondered, glancing at the large man standing in front of him.

The goon nodded once. "That's right." His arm swung back in the direction of the booth that Joey had been sitting in for the entire night.

Anthony looked at the arm and the direction that it pointed. "Thanks." He walked toward the booth and glanced back at the goon, smiling despite the fact that he was following a little closer than Anthony would have liked.

Joey was sitting in the farthest back part of the u-shaped booth. He had a cut crystal glass, half full of a white-clear liquid in front of him. As he sat holding court, Joey looked over his realm, half twisting the glass as his eyes moved around. His eyes focused on Anthony when he was only a few dozen steps away from the table. The shark smile crossed his face as he looked to his right.

A sharp jerk of his chin cleaned out the entire right arm of the horseshoe booth. All four of the people wandering away like they suddenly had something more important to do.

Joey looked at Anthony and tilted his head to the seat that was empty now, sipping his drink in a bored way.

Anthony walked up to the booth and settled into the dark chestnut, tufted leather bench and smiled a little. "You wanted to see me, Boss?"

"Oooooooooooooooooooooooooooohhhhhhh!" Olli's eyes lit up. "You got in <u>trouble</u>!"

Razor scoffed a little and shook his head. "Not exactly, Doll."

Olli frowned a little. "He literally called you over to his booth. I'm pretty sure that means you're about to get into trouble."

Razor chuckled and shrugged. "Maybe in a normal situation it would be the same as getting called onto the carpet. But...You and I both know that Joey never did anything normal."

Olli bobbed her head a little. "You'd know better than me. I never really had the distinct pleasure of meeting him in person."

Razor smiled at her in a soft way and shook his head. "Honestly, Doll. As much as I hate to say this to your face...it's better that you didn't."

Olli's eyebrows jumped up and then furrowed together a little. "What is that supposed to mean?"

Razor waved his hand a little. "I understand that insults your detective pride, but...trust me when I say that you are better off for it."

Olli leaned against the back of the chair and grunted a little. "Aces...all right. Someday you're going to have to tell me why that is." She folded her fingers together and looked at him for a moment. "So, if you weren't in trouble? What was it exactly?"

Razor grunted and shrugged slightly. "Maybe someday. And no, I wasn't in trouble..."

Joey set the glass down on the table, his hand still loosely cupped around it. "Make some good money tonight then?" he wondered, one eyebrow up slightly. He lightly spun the glass with his fingertips.

Anthony bobbed his head a little. "We had a good time." He looked up when Charley walked by and deposited a glass in front of him, swiping his empty glass in the same motion. "Thank you, Charley."

Charley smiled and nodded once. He looked over at Joey and paused for two seconds, reading his expression and his glass before walking away, back to the bar and his customers.

Joey smiled a little. "Thank you, Charley."

Anthony scooped up the glass Charley had left him and tilted his head slightly. "Why do you ask?"

Joey was after some information. Anthony wasn't going to be able to leave until he gave it. This was one of those times when it was best to just steer into the questions and get it over with.

The shark smile flashed for a moment and Joey grunted. "Not one for small talk. I like that about you, Anthony."

"You want to know how much I made tonight. Then, I imagine you're going to make me some sort of offer. I travel to all the parties you host in all your clubs, I play my game, we split the profits..." Anthony paused and seemed to weigh Joey's expression, "I'm going to guess you want something like a 70/30 split your way?" He shrugged a little and sipped his drink. "I'll counter with 60/40 split your way, you'll hem and haw a little, but eventually we'll meet in the middle and shake at the 65/35. How'm I doing so far?" He raised one eyebrow slightly and sipped his drink.

Joey sat quietly for a moment longer before he smirked. "Well. Aren't you just razor sharp?"

Olli gasped sharply and coughed once in surprise. "Is <u>that</u> how you became Razor?!"

Chapter 18
The One With The Business Deal

R azor sat still for a moment and looked thoughtful. "You know…it could very well be why he started to call me Razor." He grunted thoughtfully. "Honestly, Doll, I didn't really think about it."

Olli scoffed. "You're the only person I know that would say something like that."

Razor smirked and shrugged a little. "Do you mind if I continue with what happened next?"

Olli nodded. "Right. Sorry. Go ahead."

Anthony smiled a little and shrugged. "If you say so."

"How would you explain it?" Joey wondered, one eyebrow going up fractionally.

Anthony swirled his drink a little and shrugged. "It's not my first time on the merry-go-round?"

Joey grunted. He looked at Anthony for a moment before the shark smile was back. He scoffed quietly and shook his head. "I'd say I'm inclined to agree it <u>isn't</u> your first time on the merry-go-round."

Anthony sipped his drink. "So. How close was I?" He twisted his glass and waited patiently.

Joey looked at him for a moment, letting Anthony sweat.

Anthony picked up his glass and sipped from his drink. He looked back at Joey and waited patiently, allowing a slight smirk to cross his face.

It was time to play the game.

Joey bobbed his head a little and grunted. "I'm not sure that I've <u>ever</u> had someone lay out my entire conversation to me before I begin it."

Anthony shrugged a little. "I'm sure that you know by now that I'm not just someone."

Joey smirked and chuckled a little. "All right. Looks like there's a deal to be struck. 65/35 my way. I'll make sure that the boys that man the door to let you in like you're one of us."

Anthony's eyebrows jumped, and he made a soft, surprised noise. "That's very generous of you, Boss."

Joey sipped his drink. "It is. Isn't it?" The tone he used was proud. He was patting himself on the back.

"Aces...that <u>had</u> to be terrifying." Olli shook her head. "Nothing ever caught him off guard?"

Razor shrugged and shook his head a little. "Not that I ever saw."

Olli shook her shoulders a little. "That's something can keep you up at night."

Razor shook his head a little. "It didn't bother me. I knew we were going to make money together."

"And that's all that matters, right?" Olli tilted her head and one eyebrow went up.

Razor shook his head and shrugged a little. "In our business, that's all that really matters, yes." He stood up and walked back over to refill his glass. "Are you sure that you don't want <u>anything</u> to drink?" He pivoted to look at Olli over his shoulder slightly. "What about some coffee?"

Olli shook her head. "I really can't. But thank you."

Razor's eyebrow dipped slightly. "You say that like you haven't been here all day already." He clicked his tongue. "We both know you're thirsty. Let me get some coffee up here."

"You drink coffee?" Olli looked at him skeptically.

"What makes you think that I don't drink coffee?" Razor walked over to his desk and one eyebrow went up fractionally. He sat down in his chair and looked at her for a moment. "You could <u>at least</u> take your jacket off."

"The fact that you've <u>never</u> drank coffee before?" Olli shrugged. She hugged the jacket close to her and shook her head. "No thanks. I'll hang onto this. Can't have you handing it off to someone to have it tailored or something like that."

"Maybe not when you could see." Razor smirked. "I drank coffee just this morning." He chuckled and shook his head. "I think you'll find that the rip has been mended.

"Well. Color me impressed." Olli scoffed and shook her head a little. She opened the left side of her jacket and looked at the lining. "Well. Would you look at that?"

Razor picked up a phone receiver and pressed it to his ear. "Shh. I'm on the phone." He dialed a two-digit number and stood up straight, pushing a hand into his pants pocket. He listened to the phone and smiled at Olli calmly.

Olli clicked her tongue and rolled her eyes. She sat up a little straighter and tilted her head. "You have a <u>working phone</u> here?!" she protested, suddenly fixating on the phone.

Razor pulled his hand out of his pocket and waved at her slightly, trying to hush her with just the motion. He pulled the receiver away from his mouth slightly, covering the mouthpiece with his other hand. "Shh. Honestly."

Olli's nose wrinkled, and she tilted her head. "I didn't think there were any phone lines out here. Much less inter-building phone lines. Did we somehow end up in a high-rise downtown?"

"Hello. Coffee, please? Cream and sugar both. Yes. Thank you." He smiled and set the phone receiver down on its cradle again. He smirked at her. "No. We're not downtown in a high-rise. Though that might be something I should look into."

Olli stared at the phone for a moment like she had never seen it. "How long has that been there?"

"The phone?" Razor wondered, pointing at the phone to mimic her movement as he sat down in his chair. "Years." He shrugged and chuckled. "I thought you were a detective? Where did your powers of observation disappear off to?"

Olli shrugged. "Usually busy doing other things?" she scoffed a little. "And I never considered that it <u>actually</u> worked!"

Razor adjusted his jacket and chuckled. "You should know better."

Olli stared at the phone for a moment longer and shook her head. "Aces...you've called <u>me</u> from that phone before, haven't you?"

Razor looked at her for a moment and shrugged a little. "There is a good possibility."

Olli grunted and bobbed her head. "So that's a yes," she muttered and half shook her head.

Razor adjusted how he was sitting in his chair and smiled at her. "Coffee will be delivered soon. While we wait for our coffee, shall I continue the story?"

Olli nodded and shifted which ankle was over the other. "Sure. All right."

The next few weeks, Anthony was a regular fixture of entertainment at the parties that Joey threw. People sought out his table, ready to chase the lady and see if they could win some money.

Some were more successful than others.

Joey seemed to be pleased with the extra money that was coming in. He made sure to collect every night. A few parties in the money was exchanged over drinks in a quiet corner as the musicians for the night started to pack up.

The conversations lasted a little longer each night. Soon stretching into two or even three drinks.

Anthony melded into Joey's group, often showing up at the club with them at the same time.

Doors were really starting to open up for him.

"How long was that?" Olli wondered

"What do you mean?"

"How long did it take before you started to travel in the <u>literal</u> same circle as Joey Leftfoot?"

Razor shrugged. "Maybe six weeks?"

Olli made a thoughtful noise. "What about Teo and Eddy?" she wondered, tilting her head.

Razor smirked. "We're getting to that."

"They <u>still</u> hadn't shown up?!" Olli shook her head a little. "What were they waiting for? A mailed invitation?"

Razor shrugged a little and bobbed his head. "I'm really not sure. Maybe it just took them longer than they thought to find the parties."

Olli snorted. "Six weeks to find a mark for a con must be frustrating."

Razor grunted. "It can be. I imagine that it did make them a bit nervous."

Chapter 19
The One With The Two-Step Plan

Olli started to take a breath, but was interrupted by a soft knock on the door. She leaned over the arm of the chair that was behind her back and peered around the backrest of the chair.

A second half-hearted knock came through the door.

Razor sat up straighter. "Well. Looks like our coffee has finally arrived." He stood up and walked past Olli to the main door of the office. He opened the door and held his hands out. "I'll take it from here. Thank you."

The tray was placed in his hands and the door pulled shut.

Razor walked back to his desk and set the tray down somewhere near the middle almost to his chair. "Now. How do you take your coffee, Doll?"

Olli looked at the tray and frowned a little. "I really don't need coffee."

Razor scoffed a little and poured some coffee into two mugs. "Now, I can understand not wanting to take something from the enemy, but honestly, Doll." He looked at her and frowned slightly. "I thought we were beyond calling each other enemies." He smirked at her. "You've got to be hungry. Or at the very least thirsty. And really. Is coffee so bad?" He looked at her and tilted his head. "I won't tell anyone if you don't." He looked at her as he dropped a sugar cube into one of the cups and winked.

Olli looked at him and shook her head. "I really can't."

"I really think you <u>can</u>," Razor disagreed. He picked up the small creamer container.

Olli sighed and shook her head. "Just keep telling me the story?"

Razor added a little sugar and a light splash of cream to the coffee in the mug he had dropped the sugar cube into. He stirred it slowly with a spoon and looked at her in a half-exasperated way. "Olli, come on. Don't be like this. It would be rude of me to continue to drink and eat while you sit there stubbornly."

Olli shrugged. "Just tell me the story."

Razor sighed and sat into his chair. He reached forward and scooped up the mug and held it in his hands. "All right. The story. But drink that coffee before it gets cold will you? You really have nothing to prove."

Olli pursed her lips. "I'll think about it."

Anthony stepped out of the Cadillac sedan and buttoned the top two buttons of the three buttons on his suit jacket. He adjusted the black fedora on his head and waited patiently next to the rear door.

Next out were the two bruisers that always traveled with them. Tall, imposing, nearly always looking like they were seconds away from a bad mood. One out of each rear door. Looking around like they were expecting a threat to appear out of thin air.

Next came the blanche-complexion, thin, sharp-faced man. Joey's number two. From what Anthony had gathered over the last couple of weeks, he was the manager of the clubs as well. Two-Timer wasn't really a fan of Anthony traveling with them. He had often expressed that they were a family of money and crime.

Not a traveling circus. Whatever that meant.

Anthony didn't feel a whole lot of love for the slippery number two in the family either, but...he didn't plan on being around all that long, so it really didn't matter.

Two girls, both in bright blue and silver dresses, stepped out. Each flashed Anthony a bright smile and giggled before walking toward the club door. The hems of their dresses flouncing sharply.

Joey was the last one to step out of the Cadillac. Dressed in a deep blue, double-breasted suit with shiny black buttons. He pushed his hat onto his head and smiled at Anthony a little. "Let's go, Boys." He walked toward the club.

Anthony, the gorillas, and Two-Timer walked after him, all falling into a place they always walked.

One of the bodyguards opened the door and stood up a little straighter, looking back the way they came from, checking to make sure they hadn't been followed from the car to the door.

First the other bruiser, then the girls, Two-Timer, Joey and then Anthony walked through the door.

Once Anthony was through the door, the first bodyguard stepped around the door and followed them in, pulling the door shut behind him tightly.

"How disappointed were you when you realized that you were stuck with Two-Timer?" Olli wondered, looking at him and raising her eyebrows slightly.

Razor shrugged and sipped his coffee. "Honestly, I didn't really care. We're both businessmen. I wasn't going to stir up trouble."

"Especially when Joey gave you the best job he had to offer huh?" Olli smirked.

Razor shrugged a little and bobbed his head. "Especially then."

Olli snorted. "So he hated you already at this point." It was less of a question and more of an assumption the way that she said it. She wasn't the least bit surprised that they weren't getting along.

Razor shrugged and bobbed his head slightly. "He wasn't a fan of my traveling card show, but I don't think <u>that</u> was the point that he hated me. That came later."

Olli tilted her head, and one eyebrow went up. "Later?" Now the tone she used had a bit more skepticism.

Razor nodded in agreement. "Later at that party, in fact."

Olli sat up a little straighter and leaned close to him. "You're going to have to tell me about that."

Razor smirked and nodded. "All in good time."

Anthony pulled his hat off his head and set it on the bar top. He leaned against the edge and smiled.

"The usual?" Charley wondered, walking up and smiling a little.

Anthony smiled and nodded. "I would love the usual, actually."

Charley nodded and smiled. "You got it." He walked away and scooped up an empty, clean glass as he walked.

Anthony looked around the room and watched the people as they started to fill the place.

Looked like it was going to be quite the crowd. Already they were talking and laughing loudly. Most of them swarmed toward the coat check, shrugging out of their coats and hats. All crowding together to exchange their outerwear for a ticket.

Good night to play cards and make some money.

Good night to set his plan in action, too.

"Your plan?" Olli protested. "But I thought your plan was working already?"

Razor smirked at her. "Now-now, Doll." Razor clicked her tongue. He shook his head and sipped his coffee. "I didn't say that it was a plan with only <u>one</u> step."

Olli's eyes narrowed a little, and she tilted her head, resting her head on her hand. "Aces, that was...cryptic."

"It'll all make sense in a few minutes," Razor assured.

Olli huffed a little and nodded. "All right. Go on."

Razor smirked and sipped his coffee. "I think you're <u>really</u> going to like this next part, Doll."

Anthony stood up from the table and put his cards into the inner pocket of his jacket. It was a planned break, the crowd around him wandered away to dance and drink. They would be back to play. So would he.

It was a pattern that they had established over the last few weeks. Nothing was out of the ordinary as far as they were concerned.

Anthony walked over to the bar.

Charley was around the corner, pouring drinks and talking to patrons.

Anthony slipped behind the bar. He ducked down so no one was going to see him. He glanced to check where Charley was and reached for the phone, sitting on the shelf just at his shoulder height. After pressing the receiver to his ear he dialed a number quickly, listening to the buzz from the phone line and pursed his lips, hoping that he had just a few more seconds. There was a mob at the bar. Charley wouldn't be coming around the corner looking at anything but glasses or bottles of booze for a bit.

There was no way he was going to notice Anthony on the phone.

"Big Town Police Department."

Anthony smirked. "I'd like to report an illegal club."

Chapter 20
The One With The Finest In Big Town

O lli stared at him for a moment before inhaling a sharp breath. "You <u>called it in</u>?!" She stared at him for a moment, completely confused. "On <u>purpose</u>?!"

Razor shrugged and nodded a little. "Well sure. How else was going to solidify my place in his entourage?"

Olli blinked a couple of times. "You are incredibly devious." She clicked her tongue a couple of times and shook her head.

"This surprises you?" Razor smirked.

Olli shook her head. "No. I suppose not. It's just more...som ething <u>extra</u> devious about calling in a raid on the speakeasy that you're currently <u>standing</u> in."

Razor sipped his coffee and looked pleased. "Allllllll part of the plan." He shrugged.

Olli clicked her tongue. She shifted around in the chair, turning herself so she was sitting in it correctly. "You <u>really</u> need to stop looking so proud of yourself." She stood up out of the chair and picked up the mug of coffee that had been left, sitting on the tray, that Razor had poured for her. After adding a couple of spoonfuls of sugar and splash of cream, she used the same spoon he had to stir the coffee up a little bit. Olli lightly tapped the spoon handle on the rim of the mug before setting the spoon back on the tray.

Razor watched her and beamed a little. "It's honestly about time that you picked up that coffee. It was going to start getting <u>proper</u> cold soon."

Olli clicked her tongue and shook her head a little. She carefully sat down in the chair and adjusted herself in the seat. "So. You called Harrison and asked him to raid the building you were sitting in?" She scooted back to the far back edge of the cushion, leaning back against the backrest. "That seems a little suicidal."

Razor waved the hand that wasn't holding his coffee mug and smiled at her a little. "A means to an end." He smirked. "I wasn't worried. I had a plan."

Olli held up one hand and then all her fingers dropped down so her first finger was upright. "I have a question."

Razor raised an eyebrow. "I expect nothing else." He sipped his coffee. "What would that question be exactly?"

"The police conduct a raid...it's like shooting fish in a barrel."

"Unless..." Razor hinted.

"Unless you've had time to scope the place and know that there's more than one way out," Olli filled in the blank.

Razor nodded a little and sipped his coffee again. "There's one other thing that has to be checked too."

"Police response times."

"Well. Aren't <u>you</u> just the little gangster moll!" Razor chuckled and smirked at her.

Olli shook her head stoutly. "Not so much that. I've spent a lot of time thinking like a criminal. I get paid to, after all. It would make sense. If you don't know how long it takes for a police raid to be set up and executed or where the other exits are...the plan isn't even a <u>beginning</u> of a plan."

Razor looked at her proudly for a moment. "Well. Done. <u>Olli.</u>"

Olli sipped her coffee and smiled a little. "Why don't you continue the story?"

Razor nodded and shifted in his chair, gently resting the arm that supported his coffee on his chair. He hooked one knee over the other. "So I hung up the phone after giving the address for the club we were at that night..."

Anthony set the receiver down on the cradle and looked around to make sure that no one had noticed him, crouched like a fool behind the counter. He took a breath and stood up, snagging a bottle with his right hand as he did.

Charley stepped around the corner and stopped short. "Anthony! I'm sorry. I didn't realize you were over here! I would have poured your drink."

Anthony smirked and shook his head. He finished pouring his current drink and set the bottle back where it had been sitting. "No. It's all right. You had enough on your hands."

Charley shrugged a little and bobbed his head. "Well. I appreciate it Anthony. Just don't let the boss catch you behind the bar. You know how it is."

Anthony nodded and scoffed. "You should talk to him about getting you a second. Especially if the parties stay this busy."

Charley waved him off and shrugged. "Nah. I do just fine. But thank you for worrying."

Anthony smiled at him and stepped around the edge of the bar. "You really are a treasure, Charley."

Charley laughed quietly. "Don't tell anyone. They might think I'm some sort of pushover." He started to wipe down glasses after washing them.

Anthony laughed and started back toward the main part of the room. After a few minutes, he pulled a watch out of his pocket and looked at the time.

He had five more minutes...on the long end.

Anthony smiled to himself. He started toward the back horseshoe booth where Joey was holding court again. Hovering nearby, checking his watch a little. He had to time this just right. Too soon, and Joey would wonder how he knew it was going to happen. Too late, and Anthony wouldn't be the one to save him.

And that would make his plan go a little sideways. Nothing he couldn't recover back from, but it would take a while.

The more time he spent in Joey's inner circle, the more likely it would be that he would be found out. Anthony really didn't want to find out what it would be like when Joey found out that he had allowed a con man into his inner circle.

"Wait. There's a flaw in the logic." Olli protested.

"Beg pardon?" Razor sipped his coffee.

"How in the world would Joey <u>not</u> know you were a conman?" Olli tilted her head. "I mean really, Razor. The man had you traveling with him...running a card game." She shrugged a little. "He knew you were a conman."

"I don't—"

"You literally spoke <u>for</u> him while making a deal to split the profits." Olli shrugged a little and folded her hands around her coffee mug. "He knew exactly what you were. I've heard a lot of things about Joey, not a single one of them that he couldn't spot a conman until it was too late."

Razor looked at her for a moment before slowly smirking. "Look at the top-notch detective. Alan must be so proud," his tone was genuinely proud.

Olli pursed her lips for a moment and nodded a little. "He doesn't say very often, but I like to think he is."

"He is. You wouldn't be in the position you are if he wasn't," Razor assured.

Olli smirked and bobbed her head. "Maybe he just can't get anyone else to stick around."

Razor chuckled and nodded. "I suppose that's a possibility." He sipped his coffee and shrugged. "Though I doubt very much that it's even <u>remotely</u> probable."

"What happened next?" Olli sipped her coffee, smiling softly to herself.

"I waited for Big Town's finest to kick the door in."

Chapter 21
The One With The Raid

T he party was moving along like it always did.

Loud music, people dancing, the drinks flowing brightly.

Cigarette smoke hung thick in the air, just like nearly every night.

Charley was nearly up to his eyeballs in drink orders, barely able to keep up with the constant flow of people in front of him.

It all changed in a blink of an eye.

The front door banged open, blue uniforms and white hats pouring into the room like a swirling river.

Screams of surprise and terror echoed over the music, though the music cut out just a few seconds later.

Anthony started a little, despite himself. He pivoted and rushed over to the horseshoe booth. "Boss, you need to leave. We need to leave _now_."

Joey looked past him at the commotion thundering near the door. "What in the blazes is going on?"

"It's a _raid_, Boss." Anthony looked over his shoulder. "We need to go _now!_"

One of the gorillas nodded and waved at them. "Come on. We need to leave."

The handful of people sitting in the booth poured out and stepped out of Joey's way in a seamless motion.

Joey stood up and walked to his left, the small group trailing after him in a tight knot.

Anthony stayed behind for a moment, checking to see just how many policemen were going to come through the door. He watched them move around the room, waiting to enact the rest of his plan.

It wasn't long before someone noticed him. They pointed and yelled something that wasn't discernible through all the chaos and rushed toward him.

Anthony waited a bit too long and then sprinted away from the direction that Joey had gone. He resisted the urge to look the direction that Joey had gone.

Don't give the boss away.

That was the worst possible way to blow up a plan.

"<u>Aces!</u>" Olli set her mug down on her leg. "Let me get this straight. You set the whole thing up, and then didn't even go <u>with</u> him?"

"I was a sacrificial lamb! That's <u>important</u>." Razor shrugged slightly, a small smirk crossing his face.

"What." Olli stared at him. "Do you hear yourself right now?"

Razor chuckled. "I knew he wasn't out of the room yet. He sees me distract cops for him..."

Olli laughed. "Did you get away?"

"Oh. I did more than <u>that</u>."

Anthony took a flying leap and slid over the bar top, dropping on his feet, and crouched behind the bar. He took two steps and pulled up a four-board trapdoor. He quickly dropped down into the dark underground hole, pulling the trapdoor shut behind him.

Three—no, four—steps down and his feet landed on the floor. A quick pivot and he walked down a short hallway. Once his fingers hit the brick wall in front of him, Anthony started to feel around. There was a certain brick he was looking for. It was about middle-chest high, just a few inches to the left of center.

All he had to do was find it in quick order and he would be able to slip away, and no one would be the wiser.

A soft scraping groan came from the wall in front of him. A small, half door pushed inward. It was just big enough to slip through if Anthony went sideways.

Once through the door, Anthony closed the door behind him and paused for a beat. He didn't trust turning on the small row of lights that were probably strung somewhere. No reason to give away where he was if the police running around on the floor above him manged find their way into the underground room.

Anthony walked along the hallway, his fingers running along the wall, keeping him from running into the far edge of a corner. There were more turns in this tunnel than a snake trying to get somewhere.

Four more turns and a slight ramp up, and Anthony all but ran into a metal ladder. He ran his hand up the edge and tracked down a rung. Once he figured out the spacing, he started to climb up the ladder as fast as he could manage.

Anthony pushed up on the manhole cover and looked around to make sure that no one was around. When he was satisfied that the alley was empty, he pushed the cover up far enough that he could finally climb out of the manhole he was in. He carefully set the cover back down on the hole and stood up. He brushed off his hands on his pants. A distasteful look crossed his face.

Dirt didn't bother him all that much. Dirt grew grapes that made wine and the grains that were needed to make pasta.

Slimy grime on the other hand...there was no room in Anthony's life for it.

And that cover was horrific.

Had he been alone; Anthony would have spent more time cleaning his hands off—most likely in a sink somewhere—but there were greater things at play that needed to be taken care of. He could wash his hands properly later.

Anthony pivoted and jogged down the alley quickly. Around the first corner to the right, the large Cadillac sedan was parked in deep shadow, waiting until Joey was ready to go home. He raced up to the driver's door and jerked it open.

"We're out, Boss. You stay here out of the way, just stick to the shadows. We'll get the car and get you out of here," one of the gorillas informed, holding his hand out slightly in a protective sort of motion, looking around skeptically.

Their party had split up and fractured on the way to the alley they were currently standing in. All in an effort to make sure the boss didn't get swept up in the raid. It was only Joey and this bodyguard that were left. Which meant that Joey would be left alone while the car was fetched.

Joey nodded. "Be fast about it." He looked back the way they had come from. "Sounds like they're getting close."

There were a few yells. And sirens bounced off the walls of the buildings around them.

The bodyguard nodded. "You got it, Boss."

A black Cadillac roared up and slammed to a stop just shy of them.

Anthony stuck his head out the window. "Get in. You there." He jerked his head toward the gorilla. "You know how to drive this contraption, right?" he pointed at the bruiser as he stepped out.

The gorilla nodded and stepped toward the open door automatically.

Anthony walked away from the driver's door and pulled the rear door open. "You first, Boss."

Joey looked at him and smiled a little. "Thank you, Anthony." He walked forward and stepped into the Cadillac.

Anthony held the door open and waited until he was out of the way before swinging into the car after him. He jerked the door closed behind him with a sharp snap. "Drive man! <u>Drive</u>!"

Chapter 22
The One With The Visitors

The rear tires of the Cadillac spun and squealed sharply.

Anthony stumbled a little and half rolled into the backseat. He pulled himself up and sat on the back seat. Close to him, but not so close that he would be able to touch him. Anthony adjusted how he was sitting so he was leaning against the backrest. He adjusted his suit jacket and smiled. "Well. That was certainly exciting."

"How did you get out of the club so fast?" Joey wondered, looking at Anthony and tilting his head slightly. "You didn't leave with us. I thought I saw you cause a diversion for me."

Anthony looked at him and shrugged a little. "I did."

Joey stared at him and waited patiently in silence.

"I happened to be fast enough to beat them to the bar. Got through the trapdoor. Took the alley out and came up behind the building just a block from the car." Anthony shrugged, running his fingers through his hair, trying to put it all back in place. "When I saw it, I figured you would be needing it still and that you'd be coming out where you did."

"And you just...took it upon yourself." Joey clarified, his tone even and deathly calm, despite the wild ride they were taking.

Anthony nodded. "Can't have the boss getting caught up in a raid." He adjusted his suit coat a little again and brushed off the sleeves.

"How very considerate of you." Joey nodded slowly, looking at him steadily.

"Why'd you stop?" Olli wondered, an eyebrow going up a little.

"You're dying to ask a question." Razor shrugged and sipped his coffee. "Go ahead."

Olli nodded a little. "I was just curious how you knew where he was going to be? Did you dry run the tunnels to see which he was more likely to take? How? Who told you were all the openings were?"

Razor held up a hand and shook his head a little. "One question at a time!" He chuckled. "Suffice to say, I hear things. And apparently, they usually took him the exact same way every time unless they couldn't for some reason."

"You know, there's no real shame in just saying that you guessed, and just happened to be right that time." Olli smirked and sipped her coffee.

"Educated assumption," Razor allowed with a half shrug.

Olli smirked again and shook her head. "Sure." She sipped her coffee slowly. "Is that the point that he started to call you Razor then?"

Razor shrugged a little. "I'm sorry, Doll. He didn't start calling me that for a while."

Olli scoffed a little and didn't seem too worried. "All right. That's fine. What happened next?"

Razor made a thoughtful noise. "I think, if you don't mind, I'll skip ahead a few weeks?"

Olli nodded and smiled. "Aces. I'm not sure why you're asking me for my permission. I insist."

Razor chuckled. "All right. I finally saw my friends from the train, maybe three weeks later."

"At the same spot?" Olli wondered curiously.

Razor shook his head. "No. After the raid, Joey left the building closed for a while. Let it cool down."

"Olli nodded. "Sure. That makes sense."

Anthony relaxed back into a plush, blue, crushed velvet chair sat in a half-lit corner of a hazy, dark room.

The ceiling was low, but not close enough to create a claustrophobic feeling. The wood was dark-stained, the panels running from floor to ceiling.

It felt like an old-world cigar lounge. Smoke hung thick across the ceiling and rolled up the pillars.

Jazz came quietly from the other end of the long, oddly octagonal room. It was a smaller band than normal, but that didn't make the music sound any less smooth. They were playing a slow swing tune, watching their fingers and the dancers in a back-and-forth sort of way.

Anthony puffed on the cigar that a cigarette girl had dropped off for him a few minutes before. He had just given up his card table for a little while so his table could be used as part of the dinner service that was being set out.

Joey had insisted on having dinner while they were there. It wasn't something that had never been done in a speakeasy that anyone had mentioned to Anthony. It was a touch that made Joey's customers feel like they were really part of an in-crowd. Something that made Joey's clubs a place that <u>everyone</u> wanted to be a part of.

It was hard <u>not</u> to feel special when you were dining in the same room as Joey Leftfoot.

Anthony thought it was an incredibly smart idea.

Olli shook her head a little. "That <u>is</u> smart. It's so much easier to convince people to owe you favors when you're feeding them.

Razor nodded. "I've found this myself."

Olli smirked. "Something you've kept over from the old king then?" she wondered.

Razor shrugged. "I suppose you could show up and see…"

Olli nodded slowly and scoffed. She sipped her coffee and shifted in her chair. "All right. What happened next?"

"I just waited until dinner was done."

"I wondered where you had wandered off to."

Anthony looked up and smiled a little. "Well hello, Boss." He shrugged and hefted the cigar a little in an explanation. "Thought I'd sit over here to make sure I didn't ruin anyone's appetite."

"That's very kind of you." Joey sat in a matching chair, tossing one knee over the other. He pulled out a cigar that was a lot like the one that Anthony currently held between his lips. "Mind if I join you?"

Anthony shook his head. "No. Of course not. It's your place. You do whatever you like." He reached into his suit jacket and pulled the lighter out of the inner pocket. "Light?" He tossed it to Joey.

Joey caught the lighter. "Thank you." He smirked a little and lit the cigar.

"Boss?"

Joey looked up at one of his bodyguards. "What is it?" He pushed the cigar between his lips and took a short puff.

"There's two men here to see you, Boss."

Joey puffed on his cigar. "Do I know them?" he wondered, his voice slightly confused. He adjusted his cigar between his fingers and rested his arm over the armrest of the chair.

"I don't think so."

"You don't...think...so." Joey looked at him for a moment without doing anything. "They didn't mention what they wanted, did they?"

The bruiser shook his head a little. "Sorry, Boss."

Joey pursed his lips a little. He pondered for a moment before nodding once. "All right. Bring them over."

Anthony puffed on his cigar and smiled when the gorilla glanced at him. "Want me to push off, Boss?" he wondered, starting to lean forward like he was going to stand out of his chair.

Joey pashawed and shook his head sharply. "Sit." He waved his hand slightly to keep Anthony in his chair. He brought the cigar up to his lips and puffed on it. "This should be interesting."

Anthony froze and smiled a little. He sat back into the chair and smiled a little. "If you're sure, Boss."

"I am." Joey nodded. "I think I might need your impressions of these men that want to talk to me."

Chapter 23
The One With The Kernel of Truth

Anthony relaxed back into his chair and nodded. "You got it, Boss."

Joey looked across the club and watched the people. "Wonder what <u>this</u> could be about..."

Anthony shrugged a little. "Guess we'll find out in a minute."

Joey grunted and waited patiently.

Anthony puffed on his cigar a little and blew the smoke toward the ceiling. "This is a new thing..."

Joey shook his head. "Nah. People come to me all the time. I'm like the uncle everyone needs when they want a little something."

Anthony grunted a little and looked across the room. He puffed on his cigar and bobbed his head.

The gorilla walked back toward them. Behind him walked two men with simple, dark suits.

"Guess we're about to find out what these two need." Joey shifted in his chair.

Anthony leaned slightly, and one eyebrow tilted. He looked back at Joey and cleared his throat. "Are you <u>sure</u> you don't want me to get scarce, Boss?"

Joey looked at him and nodded once. "Anthony. No need to continue to ask. I said yes. Now leave it as that."

Anthony pursed his lips and nodded once. "Right. If that's what you want, Boss."

Olli looked delighted and giggled softly. "You got in trouble!"

Razor shrugged slightly and bobbed his head. "A little. I just wasn't sure that he would want me around while someone was pitching him an idea."

"You were officially part of his inner circle, huh?" Olli sipped her coffee.

Razor smirked. "You should have <u>seen</u> the look on their faces, Doll." He laughed a little and puffed on his cigar. "<u>Priceless</u>."

The gorilla stopped at the alcove. "As requested." He gestured vaguely to the two men that were following him.

Joey smiled a little. "You can go. I'm sure they don't mean me any harm."

After a quick nod, the bodyguard walked away, stopping to sit in a chair that was still close, but out of the way.

Two men stood in front of the alcove. One with a briefcase in hand, and the other with a self-assured smirk.

"Joey Leftfoot, I presume?" the one with the smirk assumed.

Joey looked up at him and tilted his head a little. He puffed his cigar a little and looked over the men with a cool look. "And you would be...?"

"My name is Teo. And this is my partner Eddy," the one with the smirk introduced, not the least put off by the cool demeanor.

Joey nodded a little and looked them over. "I hear that you wanted to talk to me."

Teo smiled and dipped his head. "If you have time?"

Joey spent a couple of seconds evaluating Teo. "Do I have time, Anthony?" He looked over at Anthony and raised an eyebrow slightly.

Anthony pinched the cigar between his lips and fished a silver pocket watch out of the small pocket in his waistcoat. He clicked the cover open and looked at it. "Sure, Boss." He clicked the pocket watch closed and shrugged. "It's about an hour until dinner."

"Wonderful. Thank you, Anthony." Joey smiled at him slightly. "Please. Pull up a chair and sit." He gestured vaguely to the chairs that were just outside the alcove he was sitting in.

Two sets of eyes turned and looked at Anthony.

"<u>Anthony</u>?" Teo wondered, tilting his head and blinking.

Anthony smiled and puffed his cigar. "Evening." He pushed the watch into the waistcoat pocket it belonged in.

Teo blinked a couple of times and scoffed. "I didn't realize <u>you</u> would be here."

Anthony smirked. "I didn't realize you would be here either, Teo."

"Anthony? You know these two?" Joey looked at Anthony and raised an eyebrow fractionally.

Anthony shrugged and smiled a little. "Just met on the train, Boss."

Joey nodded a little and gestured to the two chairs that were unoccupied in the alcove. "Sit down, gents. I insist."

"You didn't mention that you knew him on the train, Anthony." Teo smiled and stepped over to the first of the two chairs and claimed it for himself.

Anthony shrugged. "You never asked."

Eddy looked at him and tilted his head a little as he took the other chair. He set the briefcase on the ground next to his chair.

Anthony smiled a little. "Eddy."

"Hiya, Anthony," Eddy mused quietly.

Joey smirked a little and puffed on his cigar. "Well. This <u>is</u> an interesting turn of events. Met on the train..."

"We actually met in line before the train," Teo piped up, almost seemingly too eager to create more of a connection with Joey at Anthony's expense.

Joey made a noise of interest. "I see. Anthony? Your friends are good people?"

Anthony shrugged a little. "Sure, Boss."

"We're excellent people," Teo assured.

Joey looked over at him and grunted a little. He looked at Anthony for a moment.

Anthony nodded slightly and puffed on his cigar.

Joey dipped his chin and turned back to the newcomers. "What would you like to talk about, Teo?"

Olli covered her mouth with her hand before rubbing her jaw. "Good thing you told him your name was Anthony."

Razor chuckled and nodded. "It <u>did</u> work out in my favor that time."

Olli snorted and made a thoughtful noise in the back of her throat. "What happened next?"

"They pitched their idea to him. Told him all about the restaurant that they thought he'd like. All the plans that they had, the food and the feeling of it." Razor shrugged and gestured slightly in a vague way. "That's about the size of it."

"Did he bite?" Olli tilted her head. She sipped her coffee and waited.

Razor shrugged. "He told them he would think about it. Shooed them off to enjoy dinner. Even offered it on the house."

Olli smirked and grunted a little. "So he really wasn't interested in playing the rich uncle to them."

Razor chuckled. "No. I suppose he really wasn't. Not at first."

Olli sipped her coffee again slowly and raised an eyebrow fractionally. "At first?"

"I might have convinced him to think it over a little more."

"Why? They were competing with you for the money you wanted..."

Razor chuckled. "I wasn't too worried the money would dry up."

"Why?"

"Joey Leftfoot, Doll." Razor shrugged. "It was the '20s. He was raking money in. And he was a savvy businessman."

Olli nodded a little. "Sure. Sure..." She looked at him for a minute and grunted.

"Surprisingly, he made most of his money by investing."

Olli sat up a little straighter. "What?"

Razor nodded. "It's true. He really did."

Olli sipped her coffee again. "I really am surprised..."

"Why?"

Olli started to take a breath before pausing and tilting her head. "He did honest work?"

Razor shrugged. "It's just like every other con. Right? Kernel of truth?"

Olli sucked her teeth for a moment and scoffed. "Kernel of truth..."

Chapter 24
The One With The Paperwork

Olli looked at him for a moment and pursed her lips. "I just don't understand. When you started the story, you made it sound like you were going to compete with them for the money. And now...it just doesn't sound like that?" She tilted her head slightly.

Razor shrugged. "My plans might have changed a bit by the time the two of them walked into my life again."

Olli tilted her head. "You didn't plan on selling him the tower anymore?" She held her hands out. "But...aces, Razor. You told me that you sold him the tower of Pisa." She arched an eyebrow.

Razor chuckled a little. Almost enjoying the confusion Olli was steeping in. "Hold on. Just let me get through this part. And it'll all make sense." He assured, holding up a hand slightly and pumping it a little.

Olli set the empty coffee mug just past the edge of the desk closest to her and nodded a little. "All right." She sat back into her chair, hooking one leg over the other. "Dazzle me, Razor."

Razor chuckled and smirked at her.

Joey sat quietly for a moment after Teo had finished talking. He looked at the two of them quietly before nodding once. "Thank you, gentlemen. You'll know my decision soon."

Teo blinked. "Soon? How soon? What's not to like?"

Anthony cleared his throat a little. "It's almost dinnertime, Teo. Maybe we could talk about it after?"

"Anthony's right. We pitched it to him. Let's let him think about it, Teo." Eddy interceded, looking at Teo pointedly.

"Go, take a seat at the table. Enjoy the dinner. It's one of my favorites," Joey invited, using the hand that wasn't holding his cigar.

Teo looked like he wanted to protest for a moment.

Eddy stood up and smiled. "Thank you so much for the time. Thank you so much for your dinner invite. We're <u>very</u> grateful. Teo. Let's go get a chair at the table." He stepped toward the opening of the alcove and shot Teo an obvious hinting way that he should follow.

Teo resisted for a second before nodding and smiling a little. "Thank you." He stood up and walked toward the dinner table just a couple of steps behind Eddy.

Joey puffed on his cigar and watched them go.

"The meatballs are especially delicious." Anthony informed before they were too far away.

Eddy smiled and nodded once. "Thank you, Anthony." He caught Teo's sleeve again and tugged on it to try to get him to follow.

Teo walked after him, but looked back at Anthony like he couldn't believe that he was still there, and in such a prominent place.

Joey took a sip of his drink and watched them go. "What do you think, Anthony?"

Anthony watched after Eddy and Teo before looking at Joey and tilted his head a little. "I'm sorry?"

"What do you think of that pitch?" Joey gestured vaguely to the alcove and after Teo and Eddy.

"I don't think it really matters what I think." Anthony adjusted his suit coat and pushed the cigar between his teeth. "I think it matters what <u>you</u> think."

"Well. That was very diplomatic of you." Joey smirked a little and raised an eyebrow. He looked at the stub of his cigar and tapped the bit off the ash off the end of it into a nearby cut-glass ashtray.

Anthony shrugged a little and nodded. "Thank you, Boss."

"Now that you've said all the right things, how about you tell me what you <u>actually</u> think of what they suggested?" Joey looked at him and raised an eyebrow.

Anthony shrugged. "I think it sounds like a great plan."

Joey puffed on his cigar. "Do you."

Anthony grunted. "You don't? It's well thought out. Smacks of the old country. You'd make a killing with those of us fresh off the boat."

"I think it sounds like a scheme to get some of my money."

Anthony chuckled softly. "Every business is an outlay of money, Boss."

"It's not like they're offering me the chance to buy the tower of Pisa."

Anthony chuckled quietly and cleared his throat. "I might be able to help with that, actually."

Olli gasped sharply. "That's how you got the idea!"

Razor nodded and tapped his nose. "I honestly wasn't thinking of pulling a con. Just...fell in my lap." He shrugged. "Sometimes the best opportunities just...fall into your lap."

Olli nodded a little and grunted. "All right. Now we're getting somewhere." She rubbed her hands together. "That sounds like something dear old dad would say."

Razor smirked. "Dear old dad," he repeated, though there wasn't much warmth in the words. "You're not wrong."

Olli nodded. "So what happened? You saw the chance to help Joey make a lot of money and just jumped?"

Razor chuckled and nodded. "I thought I'd help Joey make a bit of money, and help myself to some of it in the process."

"How so?" Olli raised an eyebrow slightly.

Razor smirked and tapped his nose.

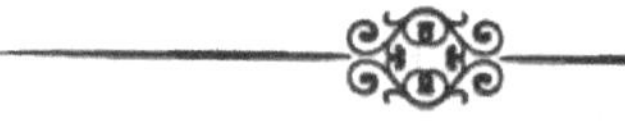

Anthony sat where he was for a moment, looking at the smoke curling off the tip of his cigar. "Really."

Joey nodded. "Are you kidding? Owning something like that?" For a moment, a far away look flashed across his face. He chuckled and sighed. "Now there's a piece of home I'd like to have."

"I might be able to help with that."

Joey tilted his head and raised his eyebrow. "Can you now?"

Anthony nodded. "I can, in fact."

"How could that possibly be?" Joey scoffed, puffing his cigar and shaking his head a little.

Anthony shrugged. "I might just have a..." he paused like he was searching for the right word. "Controlling interest in the Tower."

Joey looked at him for a moment and laughed quietly. "Anthony. You are an entertaining fellow." He shook the hand holding the cigar at Anthony and smirked. "You really had me there for a moment. I thought that you were serious."

Anthony smirked a little. "Thank you, Boss. But what if I told you that I could prove it?"

Joey puffed on his cigar and looked at him in a close, guarded way. "You can prove it," he repeated.

Anthony nodded. He sipped his drink. "I can."

"Explain." Joey blew a mouthful of smoke toward the ceiling and processed for a moment. "I think I would very much like to see that proof."

Anthony grunted. "How about I bring it by tomorrow?"

Joey nodded. "Bring it by before open. Two hours before. I have a feeling we're going to have a lot to discuss."

Anthony nodded once. "You got it, Boss."

"Two hours before open...isn't that five the next night?" Olli tilted her head and looked slightly confused.

Razor nodded. "Very good, Doll. That's exactly what it is."

"If you had only just decided to run this con, you didn't have paper to prove what you said. How were you going to get all that together by the time you needed to meet him?!"

Razor smirked. "I can work quickly. And I do my best work under tight deadlines."

Olli made a thoughtful noise. "How does that tie into the restaurant idea that Teo and Eddy pitched?"

Razor waved his hand a little. "Give me a minute. I'll all make sense."

Chapter 25
The One With The Surprise Offer

A nthony waited patiently while Joey looked over the paper-work that sat on the table in front of him.

They were sitting in the empty club under the hardware store on 25th street about an hour and a half before the club was supposed to open for the night.

"The hardware on 25th?!" Olli's voice cracked in shock. "There's a <u>club</u> under it?! How do you find it?!" She pressed her hands against the sides of her face. "How have <u>I</u> not found it?!"

Razor tilted his head and looked at her for a moment. "Is that really what you want to focus on at this moment?"

Olli blinked a few times, processing the question. "No. No. But we're going to have to come back to that."

Razor chuckled. "All right. Remind me and we'll talk about it at a later time."

"You're just going to tell me where it is? And how to get to it?" Olli tilted her head.

Razor chuckled. "Of course. It won't hurt anything."

Olli scoffed. "You don't know that."

"True. I suppose that's true. But, it could save your life one day. And that's important."

"That's very generous of you." Olli shifted in her chair and cleared her throat. "What happened next?"

Razor shrugged. "He read the paperwork over."

"How long did it take him total?"

"About a half hour."

Joey reached over for his glass blindly while he read and took a sip from it. The pour he had sat down with at the beginning of the meeting about half gone.

Anthony looked around the empty room and allowed himself to be distracted by Charley moving around behind the bar. It was more interesting to watch than the empty room. He didn't want to look like he was impatiently waiting for Joey to finish reading.

If he rushed the mob boss, there was a chance that Joey would notice things weren't exactly...real.

Charley had finished pulling all the chairs off the tops of the tables and had moved to making sure everything behind the bar was set. He was whistling to himself as he worked, towel thrown over his left shoulder like always.

"This is all very interesting, Anthony," Joey finally spoke up.

Anthony blinked and looked over at him. "Thank you." He smiled, instantly back into the present, and focused on what Joey was saying.

"This all looks very well documented. I'm impressed with how far you can trace your roots."

Anthony smiled and bobbed his head. "My family goes back a long way. We're very fortunate."

"Why did you decide to come to America, then?" Joey leaned back against the side of the booth and looked at him expectantly.

Anthony shrugged. "I was feeling a bit restless. Thought it was as good a time as any to go on an adventure."

"And you're willing to sell this to me?" Joey tapped the small stack of papers with one finger and looked at him suspiciously. "Why?"

"Honestly," Anthony shrugged. "If I'm to stay here for a while longer, I'm going to need some walking around money."

"And you're willing to sell off part of your heritage to do it?" Joey sipped his drink again.

"At the risk of sounding...pretentious..." Anthony shrugged and gestured to the papers between them. "This is only two shares that we're talking about." His shoulders twitched again. "That's not even a fraction worth <u>mentioning</u> of the shares that I have in the Tower."

Joey made a thoughtful noise. "And you're happy with this price you've proposed?" he looked over Anthony's face closely, like he was checking his reaction.

Anthony had to be careful now. This was the point where Joey was going to really start to feel out if this was all a very real thing.

This was the time when the con could die...and so could Anthony, if Joey was insulted enough.

Too late to turn back now.

Anthony nodded. "That should hold me over for a month or two. I figure I can reevaluate my need for adventure at that point."

Joey nodded. "How many shares did you say this price was for again?"

"Two."

Joey grunted and looked at the paperwork again.

Anthony didn't make a noise, just patiently waiting for Joey to ask a question or agree to the terms.

It seemed like the silence was stretching on for a bit longer than he had anticipated.

Joey cleared his throat. "What would it take to get three more shares, Anthony?"

Anthony blinked. It wasn't the question that he thought he was going to be asked. He had planned to haggle the price down a bit, purposefully setting the price incredibly high to start, just so he could have a nice tidy sum when they _did_ settle.

This wasn't something that he had planned on. Apparently, it had shown on his face before he had the chance to school it.

Joey chuckled. "I'm sure that you weren't planning on selling so many, but maybe this way you can stay a bit longer."

Anthony cleared his throat and adjusted how he was sitting. "I guess I hadn't really expected to sell five."

Best to be honest at this moment. The expression was all over his face already. And luckily enough, the mob boss thought it was over the number of shares being sold, not the fact that he hadn't anticipated the question being asked in the first place.

Joey made a thoughtful noise and tilted his head. "Would you like some time to think about it?"

Anthony pursed his lips and tilted his head a little. The wheels in his head already spinning how he was going to whip up the next three shares and how quickly he could do it.

Joey chuckled and held up a hand. "I don't mean right this second, Anthony. Although I appreciate the level of dedication." He swirled his drink a little before smiling and shrugging slightly.

"Why don't you think about it for a couple of days and let me know what you decide."

Anthony looked at him for a moment and nodded slowly. "Sure, Boss."

"I look forward to hearing your answer." Joey slid across the bench of the booth and stood up, walking to the bar in a relaxed way.

Anthony sat where he was for a moment, processing what had happened.

It wasn't very often a con was turned on his head when he was sitting right in the middle of it.

This was going to be interesting.

"Why did you hesitate?" Olli wondered, looking at him and tilting her head slightly. "It's not like it would be all that hard to create three more shares for you. They weren't <u>real</u>."

Razor shook his head. "No. But that wasn't the point either. Hesitation gives the story credibility. Plus—"—he sipped his drink and shrugged a little—"I had already given over any chance I had to jump at the offer when Joey saw how surprised I was at it."

Olli nodded and made a thoughtful noise. "Sure. That makes sense."

"It also gave me the chance to think a little more about how I was going to proceed. Did I just want more money? Or did I want to work out a different sort of deal?"

"What did you decide?" Olli wondered, tilting her head slightly. "And did you tell him right away that night?"

"I actually didn't tell him that night." Razor shook his head. "I did what he suggested I do. I took a couple of days to think about it.

Chapter 26
The One With The Sitdown

Anthony walked up to a boring-looking door and knocked once.

The door opened, and one eye looked at him suspiciously.

Anthony started to take a breath, more than ready to give the password that was required. He smiled when the door opened more, very nearly offering him enough room to slip through had he been determined enough. "Evening."

"Welcome back. Boss is here already. Back in his booth." The door swung open the rest of the way and a large man gestured for him to go ahead.

Anthony smiled and clapped his arm gently as he walked by. "Running a little late today," he explained, without being asked why he didn't come in with the boss earlier.

The big man didn't seem to care about the information, and the barest of smiles crossed his face. He closed the door tightly.

Anthony walked down the hallway and lightly tugged on the sleeves of his suit coat. It was a beautiful night. He had opted not to take a coat. Once he walked back through the last doorway into the quiet club room, Anthony pulled off his fedora and offered it to the coat check girl that had just arrived. He smiled and winked at her. "Keep that company for me, will you?"

The girl giggled softly and nodded. "No need for a number. I know who you are."

Anthony smiled brightly and dipped his head. "I feel so special now! Thank you."

The coat girl giggled and smiled in a flirty way. "You <u>should</u>."

Olli's mouth dropped open in an excited, elated way. "She liked you!"

"You'll find that happens quite often." Razor smirked and winked at her. "You should spend some time with me outside of this office."

"I think that you forget that we're not <u>actually</u> supposed to be friends." Olli looked at him and laughed a little. "Tell me what happened next?"

"It's a pity, really. I think we could really have a wonderful time." Razor looked at her and shook his head a little before sipping his drink. "So I moved further into the room..."

The band was just starting to tune up.

Charley was behind the bar already, polishing glasses and checking bottles to make sure they were ready for the night.

Anthony walked over to the edge of the bar and leaned his elbow on it. "Evening, Charley," he greeted as he lounged himself back into the bar with his lower ribs, his right forearm holding all his weight on the bar top. He looked over the empty room for a moment before smiling over his shoulder at Charley.

Charley looked over at him and smiled. "Ah! Anthony. Let me get you a drink. Boss got here just a couple of minutes ago. Holed up in the back corner over there." Charley nodded toward the back of the room and slightly to the right.

Anthony pivoted a little and glanced in the direction that Charley indicted. "Perfect. Thank you, Charley."

Charley smiled and set a glass down on the bar top. "There ya go, Anthony." He smiled quietly.

Anthony picked up the glass and smiled. "Thank you, Charley." He dropped a couple of bills on the bar and smiled. "Warm a table up for me, will you?"

Charley took the money and nodded before rolling into his sleeve. "You got it."

Anthony stood up off the bar and started toward the booth where Joey was holding court. He sipped the drink as he walked and smiled at the gorillas hanging around close by.

The first one basically ignored him, looking more toward the rest of the room, waiting for it to start to fill up.

The second one stepped in front of him.

Anthony stopped short and looked at him. "What is it?"

"He's busy."

Anthony looked at him and pursed his lips a little. "I wasn't planning on interrupting for very long..."

"Is that Anthony?" Joey wondered, leaning forward.

The brute turned halfway and looked at him. "Yeah, Boss."

"Let him through. You don't have to stop Anthony." Joey smiled, though there was no warmth in it. "Anthony is one of us."

The man nodded once and stepped out of Anthony's way.

Olli's eyebrows jumped up, and she smirked a little. "Ohhhhhh. You were one of <u>them</u>!" She smirked. "That must have made you feel really good."

"I was certainly on the right path." Razor smiled and nodded.

Olli scoffed a little. "All right. So. You must have had a plan."

"What makes you say that? I could have been just walking up to say hello and chat about the weather."

Olli raised one eyebrow and shook her head. "Not you."

Razor smirked and bobbed his head. "You're right. I had finally come up with a plan that I thought would work."

Olli smirked a little. "Tell me."

Anthony stepped around the gorilla and smiled at him brightly. "Thanks so much, Mack." He slid into the booth when Joey gestured to the bench across from him. After flashing a bright smile around the table, he sipped his drink. "Evening everyone."

There were a few mummers of returned sentiment and smiles from around the table.

Joey smiled at him and nodded once. "Mind giving us a moment?" he wondered, looking around the table and smiling in a chilly way.

He hadn't asked, really.

There were a few nods, and people started to slip away from the table.

Anthony stood up and allowed a couple to slip away. He offered a hand to two bright-smiling girls as they reached the end of the booth, offering each one a genuine smile. Once they were out of the way, he sat back down and scooted into the booth a little further to sit across from Joey. He reached over and pulled his glass in front of him. He took a sip and waited patiently for Joey to start the conversation.

Joey watched him and smiled again, this time a little warmer than the first when he dismissed everyone. "Anthony. I take it you've had some time to think about what I've proposed?"

Anthony nodded and swirled the liquid in his glass. "I have."

"Good. And?"

"Let me ask a question first."

Joey nodded in a good-natured way and gestured slightly with a hand for him to go ahead.

"Are you going to move forward with the restaurant idea?"

Chapter 27
The One With The Deathwish

Joey looked at him for a moment and tilted his head. "I'm not. ..sure I understand what that has to do with what we're talking about."

Anthony nodded a little. "I promise. It'll all make sense. Just humor me for a moment?"

Joey sipped his drink and regarded him for a moment before nodding a little. "I don't plan to move forward with it. I think it's a fishing scheme for some easy money. And I'm not in the habit of handing out money for nothing."

"With all due respect, Boss. That's a really bad idea."

"I beg your pardon." Joey sat up a little straighter.

The gasp that Olli made was sharp and dramatic.

Razor looked at her and blinked his eyes a couple of times. "Are you all right?"

Olli nodded. "Are you <u>insane</u>?!" she squawked. "How are you not <u>dead</u>?"

Razor shrugged. "I'm very lucky."

"I'd say." Olli smirked. "Must have had your lucky rabbit's foot in your pocket that night?"

Razor chuckled. "Shall I continue?"

Olli smiled and nodded a little. "Yes, please! I would love to know how you managed to talk yourself out of that."

"Have a little faith!" Razor smirked.

Anthony held up a hand. "I mean no offense."

"Little late for that," Joey mused, his tone dry but not malicious.

"He was right, you know." Olli nodded. "It was really late to say 'no offense'. Especially to someone like Joey."

Razor looked at her for a moment and shook his head slightly. "Do you mind?"

Olli giggled a little and shook her head. "Go on."

Anthony shifted in the seat and took a sip of the drink in front of him, completely unfazed by the remark. "I think it's something a little more than you give it credit for, Boss."

"How do you mean?" Joey wondered, leaning back against the backrest and regarding him patiently.

Anthony shrugged. "Aren't you always looking for new ways to make money?"

Joey ran his tongue over his teeth and grunted.

"Who isn't?" Anthony nodded, agreeing and assuming what the grunt meant at the same time. "And passive income is always a good thing. It's even better if it looks like a legit place on paper."

"I don't need another thing for the coppers to try to seize from me if they suddenly try to arrest me." Joey brushed off the point.

Anthony smirked and shook his head a little. "That's why it won't be in <u>your</u> name."

"Beg pardon?" Joey looked at him and raised an eyebrow sharply.

"It'll be in <u>mine</u>."

"Aces, Razor…" Olli looked at him in pure shock. "Do you have <u>no</u> sense of self-preservation when you're running a con or were you just feeling like you didn't have enough danger in your life at the moment?"

Razor chuckled. "It was a good idea. And if you would just let me get through it, I could prove it to you, just like I did to him."

Olli pursed her lips together and then bobbed her head. "Fair enough. I'm listening."

"And interrupting," Razor agreed.

Olli snorted.

Joey didn't move for a moment.

In fact, the moment stretched so long, Anthony began to wonder if Joey had heard him.

"Will it be?" Joey regarded him steadily.

Anthony nodded once. "It will. You'll be a silent partner. I'll run the business, make sure that everything looks good on paper. We split the profits 60/40."

Joey listened to him and a shark-like smile slowly started to spread across his face. "Oh, will we?"

"We do and I'll sell you a total of ten of my shares in the Tower," Anthony agreed.

"Ten shares."

Olli's mouth popped open sharply before it slowly started to close. She bit her lips together and a bright look crossed her eyes. She folded her hands together tightly in her lap.

Razor watched her and looked a little amused. "Are you all right?" he wondered quietly.

Olli nodded, lips still pursed between her teeth. "I don't want to interrupt..."

"But."

"No, I'm all right. Just continue."

"Why don't you just spit out what's giving you such an itch?"

"You were playing on his greed...<u>twice</u>. In the space of <u>one con</u>!" Olli's voice pitched up so rapidly and with such force, it nearly cracked.

"That's right." Razor smirked, a proud tone in his voice.

Olli laughed a little and shook her head. "What did he say?"

Anthony nodded. "<u>Ten shares</u>."

"The restaurant idea isn't worth <u>that</u> many shares." Joey shook his head.

"Not now, it isn't," Anthony agreed, "but with a few little tweaks that I have in mind, it'll be worth at <u>least</u> that."

"And you'll just willingly hand over eight more shares? Without even a little bit of a bidding war?" one of Joey's eyebrows went up fractionally.

"I didn't want to insult you." Anthony shrugged a little, swirling the liquid in his glass and glancing at Joey with a small smirk. "I figured you'd appreciate the fact that I came to you with a well-thought-out offer."

Joey looked at him for a moment and nodded his head slowly. "I suppose that's true."

Anthony grunted slightly and looked at him expectantly. "What do you think?"

Joey didn't answer right away. His eyes became unfocused, and he seemed to stare at the wall that was just to the right and behind Anthony's head for a moment.

Anthony waited patiently, allowing Joey the time to think without protest. He sipped his drink and looked over the room as the crowd started to grow.

The band struck up a lively tune.

Charley already had a line up to the bar.

It was going to be a busy night. That meant good things for the card game. Anthony would be starting up later at the table Charley had already set aside for him. A simple glance over near the far edge of the bar, and Anthony was easily able to find the table with two chairs. He nodded to himself a little.

That was a good place for it.

"Tell me what brought you to ten shares being a fair price," Joey instructed, interrupting Anthony's study of the room.

Chapter 28
The One With The Brief Intermission

Anthony focused on Joey again and he shrugged sightly. "It seemed like a good round number. It's enough start up to bring the restaurant idea to life and get it running, at least for the first little bit. Then, after that, the offer becomes <u>very</u> lucrative for both of us."

Joey nodded slowly. "What split did you say again?"

Anthony smirked, catching the trip-up question easily. "60/40 your way. All profits."

"And you're willing to stay in the States for that long?" Joey looked at him shrewdly.

Anthony shrugged. "I like it here. I have no reason to go home; after all, I'm making money."

Joey smirked. "And we all like to make money."

Anthony tapped his nose and nodded. "That we do, Boss."

"Why would I get so much of the profits? I bought your shares of the Tower..." Joey looked at him, eyeing him for any lie that he might be told.

Anthony shrugged and made sure his face didn't reveal anything. "I figure for the first year, you should have the best deal possible. After the first full year, we can sit down again and reevaluate the split. Maybe to something a bit more fair." He smirked. "Providing you like the way that I run your establishment."

Joey leaned forward and rested his arms on the table. "What makes you think that I'd consider something like that?"

Anthony smirked and leaned his arms on the table the same way. "Because you already allow me to make money here with my card game. And you don't strike me as the kind of man that would hinder a man from making more if his work deserved it, as long as you were getting a taste."

Joey made a thoughtful noise. "I'd have to think about this."

"I don't expect you to make a snap decision, Boss. Like I said." Anthony smiled a little and sipped his drink. "It's a good offer though. And you know it as well as I do."

"What if I don't want to do the restaurant, and still want the shares?" One of Joey's eyebrows moved fractionally in a challenging way.

Anthony took a long breath, thinking about the statement, and being slightly dramatic about it. He shrugged a little. "Then the restaurant idea is mine alone, and you'll have to buy into it if you want a taste."

Joey looked at him for a moment, his face completely still. "Is that so."

Anthony nodded. "And I don't think you're that foolish."

"Restaurants are a dime a dozen. What makes you think this one will be so special?" Joey challenged again.

"What makes you think it isn't?" Anthony returned almost instantly. "Seems to me you're just upset that you didn't think of the offer before I did."

Fortune favors the bold.

Joey's head pulled back slightly, and he scoffed. "Well. Aren't you just one for saying what's on your mind without any regard for the consequence."

Anthony smirked. "Make me an offer that you think is more attractive and I'll consider it."

Joey looked at him steadily for a moment.

Anthony smiled a little and shrugged. "I don't need an answer right away, just something that you'd probably want to consider thinking about before we move forward with this."

"What makes you think that it should be _me_ offering _you_ anything, Anthony?" Joey raised an eyebrow slightly.

Anthony shrugged a little. "Isn't that how negotiations work?"

"We're negotiating now?" Joey scoffed slightly. "I thought that _I_ was the boss?"

"Of course you are, Boss. If you don't like my offer." Anthony nodded. "Then that means we can start to negotiate something that both of us find appealing."

"I know how negotiations work, Anthony," Joey informed in a chilly tone.

Anthony nodded and smiled warmly. "I'm aware that you do, Boss." He sipped his drink. "And you know that I mean no offense by it." He smirked. "I'm just trying to make us both very rich men."

"I'm already a rich man."

Anthony tilted his head. "So, you don't want to make any more, then?"

Joey chuckled a little. He sat back against the booth and nodded slowly. "You know. I really like you, Anthony."

Anthony sipped his drink and made a small, thoughtful noise. "Thank you, Boss."

"Give me so time to think about it. I'll send someone to find you."

Anthony nodded a little and scooted out of the booth. "Thank you, Boss." He stood up and grabbed his glass by the top rim. As he walked away, he took a sip of his drink.

Maybe now was a good time to start setting up for the card game. It always soothed nerves when they got frayed.

And his nerves were a little more than frayed after staring down the shark and baiting him.

A hand settled on Anthony's right shoulder.

Anthony ignored the hand and turned the card over that had been chosen. "Oh. <u>No</u>! Sorry about that! Better luck next time!" He smiled as a groan rippled through the crowd, and side bets were exchanged.

The hand rested a little heavier. "Boss wants you," a gruff voice informed just a couple of seconds before the hand picked up.

Anthony looked over his shoulder and nodded a little. "I'll be right there."

"<u>Now</u>."

"Tell him I have two more hands and I'll be there." Anthony nodded and sipped his drink before setting the glass on the table. He started to shuffle the three cards in his hands, smirking at the man across the table from him. "Hope you're feeling lucky—"

The hand dropped onto his shoulder again. "The Boss isn't interested in waiting for you to finish two hands. You need to come right now."

Anthony looked at the hand on his shoulder and pursed his lips a little. "The man already paid for the next two games." He looked up at the gorilla the hands were attached to. "I'm sure the Boss will understand."

The bodyguard looked at him and gripped his shoulder. "You're coming now. I'm sure <u>he'll</u> understand."

Anthony looked at the man across the table. "Mind if we take a brief intermission? Apparently, my presence has been requested elsewhere. Here." He handed a couple of bills over and smiled. "Why don't you get us both a drink, tell Charley I'll have my usual? And I'll meet you back here for the next three games. Last one's on me." He winked and smirked.

The man smiled and grabbed both glasses and walked toward the bar.

Anthony smiled around the group and stood up from the chair. "Brief intermission folks. I'll be right back. Keep that money warm!" He turned and looked at the bodyguard dryly. "All right. Let's go."

Chapter 29
The One With The Definition Of Stupid

O lli scoffed a little and shook her head. Ever get the feeling that you're a little more brave than you should be?" She tilted her head.

"He was being rude to my customers!" Razor protested a split second before blowing his cigar smoke toward the ceiling.

"I'm not sure that Joey would have cared." Olli shrugged.

"I'm quite sure he would have. Especially since we were splitting the profits of the game."

Olli smirked and leaned back into the chair. "You don't have to be so insulted. It's been a few years. That's money's long gone."

Razor shrugged. "It's the principal of it."

Olli scoffed a little and gestured for him to go ahead. "All right. Tell me what happened next."

Anthony walked away from the card table and back toward the booth he had started the night out in. "Having a good night?" he wondered, looking at the large man next to him and smiling warmly.

The man half glanced at him and the corner of his lips moved up in the barest of seconds. "He's right over there." His chin moved up sightly and he turned to face the room again.

Anthony smiled at him and walked forward to the booth Joey had chosen for himself. "Hi there, Boss."

Joey looked up at him and smiled a little. "Anthony, so great of you to join me so quickly."

Anthony smiled tightly. "Of course, I needed a refill and to rest my wrists, anyway." He shrugged it off.

Joey looked over at the man he had set to get Anthony and shrugged a little. "Sorry about that. I told him that I wanted to talk to you soon. I had no idea he was going to take that so literally."

Anthony shook his head. "It worked out. I've got the man hooked for at least three more games. And he's honestly <u>terrible</u> at it. So we'll still get our money for the night."

Joey's shark smile was back. "Good."

"I take it you've had enough time to think about my offer and you have a counter offer ready for me?"

Joey grunted and sipped from his glass. "I have. And I don't."

"What is that supposed to mean?" Olli tilted her head.

Razor chuckled. "That's exactly what I expected you to say."

"Did you just accuse me of being <u>predictable</u>?!" Olli gasped a little, fluttering a hand in front of her face in a dramatic, southern belle sort of way.

Razor smirked. "Don't worry. I won't tell anyone."

Olli looked at him for a moment and nodded slowly. "Thanks." She smirked. "I doubt that anyone would believe you, anyway."

"I'd take that bet." Razor looked at her with one eyebrow up and put the cigar between his teeth.

Olli looked at him for a moment and clicked her tongue. "Maybe you should just continue the story."

Razor smirked. "All right."

"I'm not sure what that means." Anthony tilted his head and eyebrow went up slightly.

"Wait! If you didn't know yourself! Why did you give me a hard time about it!?" Olli interrupted again, her neck stretched out and her voice a little raspy.

Razor shook his head. "I didn't."

"You called me <u>predictable</u>!"

Razor's face hinted he might have done the whole thing on purpose, just to get a rise out of her and smirked.

Olli clicked her tongue. "All right. Go ahead."

Joey looked at him for a moment. "I think you do."

Anthony shrugged a little. "Do I?"

"I think it's a good offer."

Anthony smiled. "I thought it was too. But I'm a little surprised. I thought you'd have a counter offer."

Joey shook his head. "I thought about it. And you're right. It's a <u>very</u> attractive offer."

Olli tilted her head. "I don't understand. Why would you <u>want</u> him to counter?"

Razor shrugged. "If he wanted more shares, I could get more of the restaurant...never hurts to hope."

Olli laughed a little. "When double-dipping, it's best to dip as deep as you can?"

Razor snorted. "Something like that."

"Why do you suppose he didn't?"

Razor smirked. "About that..."

Anthony nodded. "I thought you would think so."

"And the way I see it, if we start talking about more shares, you're going to want to split the profits differently, and I'm currently in a very good way as far as profit goes."

Anthony smiled and nodded like he was aware of the information. "I thought you would like that."

Olli laughed a little. "Isn't he a shark..."

"Yeah. He thought he was clever." Razor nodded.

"Well, in his defense...he didn't think anyone would be so stupid."

"Stupid?!" Razor protested.

Olli looked at him and tilted her chin down. "Conning a mafia don...that's pretty much the definition of stupid."

Razor clicked his tongue and shook his head. "I don't think so."

"What would you call it?"

"Self-confidence."

Olli snorted and looked at him dully. "Just tell the story."

Joey made a small humming noise and nodded again. "All right. What do you say we give this a start?"

Anthony nodded and smiled. "That sounds great, Boss."

Joey made a thoughtful noise. "All right. I'll get my lawyer to start drawing up the papers."

Anthony tilted his head. "You have a lawyer? We don't need paperwork, Boss. Handshake is good enough for me."

"Not for me." Joey shook his head. "And, Anthony, only a stupid man would do business without a lawyer."

Anthony nodded a little. "Sound advice, Boss." He nodded a bit.

Olli tilted her head. "He had a lawyer? Joey Leftfoot put things on paper?"

Razor pointed at her and shook his finger a little. "Oh no. No-no. I see those little detective wheels turning." his finger spun a little in a circular motion next to his right ear. "I don't know where or if there's any <u>actual</u> paper on any or all of his business dealings." He shrugged a little. "We both know he was a bad man. He's not alive for you to attempt to bring him to justice anyway. Let sleeping dogs, Doll."

Olli folded her arms and pursed her lips a little. "So there's a chance..."

Razor shrugged. "Maybe. Honestly, I don't know, and I wouldn't help you look for them."

"Why not?"

Razor puffed on his cigar a little. He looked at her steadily for a moment and shook his head. "You're not really asking me that...<u>are you</u>?"

Chapter 30
The One With The Back Office

Olli sat there for a moment, gnawing on the inside bottom left corner of her lower lip. "Yeah. Aces...all right. Know my audience, huh?"

Razor nodded and tapped his nose.

Olli shook her head and let the silence stretch for a while. After a bit, she blew out a long breath and looked at him. "All right. When did he figure out you were conning him?"

Razor smirked. "What makes you think he figured it out?"

"Are you saying he never figured it out?" Olli's eyebrows knit together, popped apart, and one went up.

Razor shook his head a little and smirked. "I don't think he ever would have."

Olli's chin tipped slightly, and one eyebrow went up slightly. "Are you saying that someone <u>told</u> him?"

Razor chuckled and smirked at her. "I'm not saying he didn't have help."

Olli's hand slowly moved up to her mouth, and she stared at him for a long moment. "Aces...that's...<u>unexpected,</u>" she mumbled through her fingers.

Razor nodded. "My thoughts exactly."

"What happened?" Olli wondered, her voice still half-stunned.

"Joey came in one night before we opened..."

Anthony looked around the room, smiling to himself. The marble shone, polished within an inch of it's life, the bright, glazed tiles sparkled under the lights.

The band was set up on the stage, chatting in quiet tones as they got set up for the night's dinner service.

Anthony leaned on the bar top and looked over the back edge with a small smile. "Think you'll be all set, Charley?"

Charley stood up and smiled a little. "Yeah, Tony. We're almost set."

Olli's hands flew up. "I'm sorry. He called you <u>Tony</u>?!"

Razor shrugged a little. "I didn't mind."

"I didn't realize that people were allowed to shorten your name." Olli mused, like the thought both stunned and amused her.

Razor shook his head. "You will never cease to amaze me, Doll. Of all the things to focus on, you always manage to find one that I'm not anticipating."

"It's good for you."

Razor chuckled and hummed a little. "Really not the fact that I had Charley bar tending?"

Olli shrugged and shook her head. "No. That's not surprising."

Razor's eyebrow jumped slightly. "Isn't it?"

"Why would it be?" Olli wondered in the same tone. "Joey was going to want eyes and ears in the place to make sure that everything was happening like you said it was. Who better than Charley?"

Razor started to take a breath, but leaned back into his chair and laughed quietly. "Well...color me impressed."

"My little detective wheels were turning." Olli smirked, spinning her right first finger next to her right ear.

Razor scoffed and shook his head.

"The place looks good, Anthony."

Anthony looked over his shoulder and smiled brightly. "Well hello, Boss. Would you like to choose your regular table?" He stood up off the bar and gestured toward the room. "You're just in time to do it. And the band has some <u>great</u> numbers warmed up for tonight."

Joey shook his head. "We need to talk."

"Sure. Let Charley get a drink for you and we'll set up at your table and—"

"In my office."

Anthony tilted his head and nodded. "Of course, Boss." He set his glass down on the bar and smiled. "Charley? Have the table set up for him when we're finished."

Charley looked up and nodded. "You got it, Tony."

"Set the table for two, Charley," Joey spoke up.

Charley's gaze switched to Joey and he smiled. "Sure, Boss."

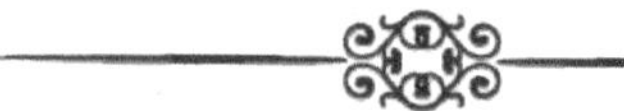

"Well. If he was having the table set for two, you must have felt better about your chances of dying from the trouble you created."

Razor looked at Olli and smirked. "Unless, of course, I wasn't the second person."

Olli looked at him for a moment and grunted. "Sure. That's a fair point." She bobbed her head a little. "Were you worried at all? When he asked to talk to you in your office? And why did he call it <u>his</u> office?"

"Technically...it <u>was</u> his office. He owned a bigger stake in the company."

Olli nodded a little and made a thoughtful noise. "So? Were you worried?"

Razor shook his head. "Not really."

Olli shook her head. "Not really? What do you mean? I'm nervous, and it was years ago <u>and</u> I have nothing to do with this."

"Good thing you weren't there then, Doll." Razor chuckled softly.

Olli shook her head and rolled her eyes. "What happened?"

Joey walked out of the main room of the restaurant and started down the back hall to the small office at the back of the building. He opened the door and let himself in when they got to it.

Anthony walked in after him.

"Shut the door."

Anthony closed the door, not looking the least bit ruffled. "What can I do for you, Boss?"

Joey walked over to the desk and sat in the chair behind it. "Why don't you sit down."

Anthony nodded a little. He walked to the chair that was closer to him, on his side of the desk and took a seat. He waited patiently.

"Anthony, were you aware that you've been lied to?"

Anthony pulled his head back slightly and tilted his head. "Lied to, Boss?"

Joey nodded. "Indeed."

"I'm not sure I understand."

"Are you aware that His Holiness, the Pope, considers himself the full and titled owner to the Tower?" Joey leaned back in the chair and waited for Anthony to say something. His shark grin was back, and it nearly chilled the room a few degrees.

Anthony looked at him for a moment. "Is he."

"Are you further aware that there has never been a family that has owned any piece of that title? <u>Ever</u>."

One of Anthony's eyebrows moved up slightly. "You don't say."

Joey watched him for a moment, fathoming out his reaction. "You don't seem surprised."

Anthony shook his head. Nothing to do but steer into it. "Honestly, Boss. I'm surprised it took you this long to find out."

Olli inhaled so sharply she started to cough.

Razor looked at her, alarm in his face. "Are you all right?!" he wondered, half leaving his chair like he was worried she might need help.

Olli held up a hand and coughed a couple more times.

Razor stood out of his chair and walked to where an open decanter with water sat on a tray next to some cut crystal glasses. "Are you sure?" he wondered, glancing over his shoulder at her while he poured some water into the glass.

Olli wheeze-coughed again. She nodded, still coughing.

Razor walked back over to the desk and set the glass down in front of her. "Here. It'll help."

Olli waved him off with one hand, her other still covering her mouth as she coughed.

Chapter 31
The One With The Long Wait

"What? You can't honestly think that I have a pitcher of drugged water in my office?!" Razor protested, his tone indigent.

Olli froze for a moment, in the middle of winding up for a cough. She stared at him and managed to raise her eyebrows.

"And that I would do something so <u>horrible</u> as to give it to <u>you</u>?!"

Olli couldn't hold the cough back anymore and coughed hard once.

Razor clicked his tongue and picked up the glass. He took two large sips and set the glass back down, where he drank on the opposite side of where Olli would drink from. "See?"

Olli coughed once and looked at him for a moment. "Aces! Fine!" she ground out, mostly through her teeth, trying to force the coughs down.

Razor shook his head. "There's no one to impress. Not here. Take a drink. It'll help."

Olli coughed one more time, almost wheezing with the effort, and reached forward the grab the glass. "Thanks," she croaked.

Razor nodded and stepped over to sit down in his chair again. "Are you going to be all right?"

Olli cleared her throat and took a sip of the water. "I'll be just fine." She cleared her throat harder and sipped the water again. "You said <u>what</u> to him?!"

Razor chuckled. "I was serious. I am actually surprised that it took him that long to find out."

"How <u>long</u> was it before he noticed?"

Razor shrugged. "Three years and five months."

Olli stared at him for a moment. "Three and half years."

Razor nodded. "Like I said. I was surprised it took him so long."

"What about the money?" Olli tilted her head. "Wasn't the whole point..." She pursed her lips. "How did he get money for the shares that he supposedly owned?" She tried again.

"Oh. It wasn't a money thing." Razor shook his head.

"Did...did you leave that out for him like you did for me?" Olli wondered, her tone dry, and one eyebrow up.

"What is that supposed to mean?" Razor wondered.

"It means that for someone who would ramble on about the stars in the sky...you sure missed a big chunk there, if that was actually the case." Olli pointed out.

Razor looked thoughtful for a moment, and then shrugged. "Must have slipped my mind."

"No." Olli shook her head. "I don't believe you."

Razor smirked. "Twice a year, I added a little extra on top of his cut."

Olli narrowed her eyes a little, clearly disappointed at the explanation. The next moment, her eyes twitched a little. "Well. That wasn't nearly as exciting as I thought it was going to be. Didn't that cut into your profits?"

Razor shook his head. "Not really. The restaurant was very profitable." He crossed one knee over the other and smirked. "Besides, I considered it part of the cost of doing business, so I really didn't miss it."

Olli nodded a little. She didn't look all that convinced, but after a moment of hemming and hawing, she gave up and shook her head. She suddenly blinked and half clicked her tongue. "Wait...aces, if that was the case, how did he figure it out?"

Razor snorted.

Joey looked at Razor for a moment, not moving. He took a couple of breaths before folding his hands together. "You want to run that past me again?" he wondered.

"I said, I was surprised that it took you this long, honestly." Razor shrugged.

"Interesting." Joey leaned back in his chair a little. "Most men wouldn't flat out repeat what they just said when I give them the chance."

Anthony shrugged. "I thought for sure you'd figure it out within the first quarter of the first year."

Joey looked at him for a moment, sitting perfectly still.

Olli's right hand shot up slightly before she swung both hands a little. "Aces...<u>how</u> are you still alive?!"

Razor chuckled. "I wasn't worried."

Olli's eyebrows knit together and her hands swung out a little. "<u>Why not</u>?!" She rested a couple of fingertips on her forehead for a moment. "I <u>am,</u> and I know that you survived!"

His shoulder bobbed a little, and he shook his head. "I don't think you understand just how much money we were raking in with my little restaurant." Razor smirked. "I banked a lot on that."

Olli took a breath and looked at him steadily. "And you figured the dollar signs would blind him to the betrayal?"

"It's not like he hadn't made the money back tenfold..."

"Mafia dons <u>are</u> known for letting water flow under the bridge on beefs a few years old..." Olli pursed her lips a little and nodded. "Just throw a few more Franklins at him."

Razor chuckled. "So I rolled the dice a little." He shook his head. "And it wasn't Franklins...so much as it was Madisons and Chases."

Olli started to take a breath and then bobbed her head slightly. "Aces. Five or ten thousand at a time probably <u>did</u> make a bit of difference..."

Razor smirked and winked.

Anthony hooked one knee over the other and waited for Joey to say something.

"See, this is normally the part where the man I'm talking to starts to sweat a bit and tries to placate me. But you're not..."

"You told Charley to set for two places. Can't eat if I'm dead." Anthony shrugged.

"Who said it was for you?" Joey wondered, his tone dark.

"Who else would it be for?" Anthony wondered. "You didn't come in with any of your goons, and you won't let anyone into the place before it opens."

"It could be for anyone. I'm the <u>boss,</u>" Joey pointed out, a hard edge on his tone.

Anthony nodded a little. He shrugged a little. "And <u>as</u> boss, your job should only be worrying about money coming in."

Joey looked at him for a moment and tilted an eyebrow.

"And have I not made you extremely rich in the last few years?" Anthony wondered, leaning against the back of the chair loosely.

Joey grunted a little. "Where's the money?"

"The share money?" Anthony wondered, his tone assuming.

Joey didn't react. He simply sat where he was and waited for Anthony to answer him.

Anthony gestured around them. "Used it for this." He smirked. "You've made all the money back and then some. It never left you. It just...moved around a little."

Joey looked at him and chuckled a little. "Find the lady, eh?"

Anthony smirked and nodded. "As you say, Boss."

"Why didn't you just start the restaurant when I didn't want to do it?"

"I came here with only a couple of dollars in my pocket. And playing find the lady in the club wasn't really making any <u>real</u> money." Anthony shrugged.

"And you thought that conning me out of the money was the solution?" Joey looked at him dully. "Why not just ask for a loan?"

"With all due respect, Boss?" Anthony leaned forward a little and smirked wickedly. "Where's the fun in that?"

Chapter 32
The One With The Job Offer

J oey sat still for a moment, looking at Anthony like he hadn't considered that option. "You did this because...it was <u>fun...</u>"
Anthony shrugged and leaned back into his chair again. He smirked. "Is there really any other reason besides the money?"

"About the money." Joey held up a finger. You say that you never had access to the Tower. And you certainly didn't make any money off holding those fake shares you sold to me...where did my bonuses come from?"

Anthony rested his arms loosely on the chair. "You really want to know?"

Joey stared at him. "If you value your life..."

"So he <u>did</u> threaten you." Olli looked almost relieved.

Razor made an indignant face. "You don't have to look so pleased, Doll."

Olli smirked and tilted her head. "I'm not <u>pleased</u>! I'm glad that the stories I heard were true, and that you didn't just have some sort of strange sway over him."

"He threatened my life on many occasions." Razor shrugged. "That just happens to be the first time that I remember him doing it."

Olli nodded. "So everything was normal."

Razor chuckled.

"What did you tell him?"

"About the money?"

"No." Olli scoffed. "About the ship that took you from Italy here to the States..."

A smirk pulled at Razor's lips.

Anthony paused a moment and nodded. "Fair enough." He shrugged slightly and relaxed into the chair further. "Cost of doing business."

Joey blinked a couple of times and slowly smirked. "The cost of doing business..."

Anthony nodded. "That's about the size of it."

Joey nodded a little and grunted. "I see."

Despite how he did his best to look on the outside, Anthony was starting to get worried. This was the point that he hoped he would never come to. And now, here he was. He had <u>had</u> a plan in place for a while for this moment, but over the last year or so, things had changed so much that the plan no longer would work.

He would have to think up something on the fly to keep from dying under the angry watch of the man across the desk from him.

Joey sat quietly, seemingly enjoying the turmoil that boiled under the surface. He loosely folded his hands together and watched Anthony waiting for him to crack.

"What happens now?" Anthony wondered a few minutes later. Sometimes, it was just better to bite the bullet and ask the question you didn't want the answer to.

This felt like one of those times.

Joey took a long breath and looked at him for a moment, his gaze dark and steely. "I'm really not sure, Anthony."

Anthony couldn't argue with that statement. He was sure that Joey was weighing the options. He was sure that the insult of being conned wouldn't be taken lightly.

However, the money would be difficult to ignore.

Joey's hands were still folded together, but he moved his fingers back and forth slowly. He looked Anthony over and slowly narrowed his eyes. "What am I going to do with you, Anthony?"

Anthony shrugged a little. "I think that's something that completely falls into your business, Boss."

Joey looked at him and narrowed his eyes. "That is the problem, isn't it? That it's my business."

Anthony smiled tightly and grunted.

"Which is where the problem comes in. You've managed to make us both a lot of money. Both with this restaurant and with that card game that you play at the clubs." Joey talked like Anthony wasn't even there. "But on the other hand, you also conned me out of a lot of money to start this place up, instead of just pitching it as a business, I wouldn't have to babysit personally..."

Anthony waited patiently, not wanting to interrupt the thought process. To do that might tip the scales in the wrong direction. He didn't want to get himself into more trouble than he was already in.

Joey made a hmmming noise as he sighed deeply.

The silence stretched for a long moment.

Anthony did his best to quell the urge to shift in his chair.

Joey had that look. The look of a shark cruising for its next meal. And Anthony was the only one that was within striking distance.

Anthony allowed himself to move his fingers a little on the arms of the chair. Waiting was starting to make him feel antsy. He wasn't surprised that Joey was letting the silence stretch so long. He probably would have done the same thing if he was in that position.

"How long did he make you wait?" Olli wondered.

Razor paused for a moment, thinking back. "Probably only just a few minutes. It felt like a whole lot longer."

Olli bobbed her head. "That makes sense. Must have been just like this story."

Razor clicked his tongue. "Now-now."

"What _did_ happen?"

Just when it seemed like Anthony was going to burst in frustration at the quiet, Joey finally started to shift.

Anthony's eyebrows went up slightly. "Well?" he wondered.

Joey smirked a little. "I've gotta say, Anthony, you are probably one of the bravest or stupidest men I've ever encountered."

Anthony shrugged. "Thank you?"

Joey smirked a little. "When I came over here, I had every intention of making sure that when I had dinner tonight, one of the girls would be joining me."

Anthony nodded slowly and grunted.

"But once I got here, it occurred to me that you probably had a plan in place for such an occasion." Joey looked at him in a piercing sort of way.

Anthony bobbed his head a little. "I would call it more of a thought than a plan..." he downplayed.

Joey grunted and nodded. "The more I think about it, the more I realize that I could use someone like you."

"Someone <u>like</u> me?" Anthony pried. "Or someone like <u>me</u>?"

Joey smirked and a short chuckle escaped him. "Nothing ever quite slips past you does it?"

Anthony shrugged a little. "I'm flattered."

"I can use someone like <u>you</u>," Joey mused a couple seconds later after some quiet. "Someone razor sharp."

"That's flattering."

"Interested in a job, Razor?"

Chapter 33
The One With The Phone Call

Olli rested her chin in her left hand, her elbow propped on the arm of her chair. She shook her head as much as she could in her hand and scoffed. "<u>Only</u> you."

Razor lifted one eyebrow slightly. "I'm not sure what you mean."

"You know, I heard that some people thought you had nine lives. Especially since no one can shut The Phoenix down...<u>that</u> had to have eaten up at least three of them."

Razor looked at her for a moment and blinked. "What?"

"Nine lives. Like a cat?"

"I'm familiar with the concept," Razor assured. "I just...had no idea that people thought that."

Olli waved her right hand a little and shrugged. "Doesn't matter. Did it shock you when he offered you the job?"

Razor scoffed. "Stopped me dead in my tracks for a moment... yes."

Anthony sat perfectly still for a moment before blinking a couple of times. "Beg your pardon?"

Joey looked at him and nodded a little. "You heard me."

"Sorry, I just...I thought I heard you offer me a job."

Joey made an agreeing noise. "That's probably because I did. Like I said. I need someone like <u>you</u>. Fearless, with a mind for business. My clubs are in a bit of tailspin lately, and I think that you're just the ticket to get them back on track."

Anthony nodded a little and looked at him for a moment. "What did you call me?"

Joey smirked, still somehow managing to make it look shark-like. "Razor." He leaned back into the chair deeply and adjusted his tie over his chest a little. "If you're going to be part of my family, I think you deserve a good name. One fitting of someone with a razor-sharp brain like yours."

Anthony smiled a little and dipped his chin. "Thank you, Boss."

Joey nodded. "Now. I think we should have dinner and discuss the terms of your new job venture."

Anthony nodded a little. "Sounds good to me, Boss."

Joey stood up and squared his shoulders a little. "After you, Razor."

"And the rest...as they say, is history." Razor smiled a little and shrugged.

Olli shook her head a little. "Just like that." She snapped her fingers.

Razor nodded. "Just like that."

"When did you start to think of yourself as Razor and not Anthony?"

Razor shook his head a little and shrugged slightly. "Honestly, Doll I'm not entirely sure when it happened, or if it completely waited for me to allow it."

Olli nodded a little.

"Well?" Razor tilted his head and raised an eyebrow. "What do you think?"

"I think that wasn't how I thought that it was going to go when you started the story. I didn't see the restaurant coming into play the way that it did."

Razor smirked and shook his head a little. "I didn't either when it started. Honestly I thought it up on the fly on my way back to my room in the boarding house."

Olli made a quiet noise and bobbed her head. "How long was it, between when you thought of it and when you pitched it to him?"

Razor shrugged a little. "Two days."

"That long?"

"I didn't see him the night between." Razor shrugged.

"Makes sense." Olli nodded a little. She let the silence stretch for a bit, looking around the room a bit.

Razor watched her for a moment and pursed his lips. "I think it's time for you to go home."

Olli took a breath and nodded in agreement. "I'd like that. I feel like I've been sitting here for two full days."

Razor chuckled and fished a pocket watch out of his waistcoat. He clicked the cover open and shook his head a little. "Sorry, Doll. You've only been here for about ten hours."

Olli blinked a couple of times. "Only ten hours..."

"It would have been shorter if you didn't continually interrupt me, you know."

Olli looked at him for a moment and shrugged a bit. "I had questions."

Razor smiled and nodded. "I'm very, _painfully_ aware."

Olli folded her arms and looked at him for a moment with a dull look.

Razor smirked and shook his head. "Don't let me keep you."

Olli blinked and shook herself a little. "Right. Time to go." She untangled herself from the chair. She stood up, grabbed her leather jacket, and started to walk to the cabinet that also just so happened to the doorway to the tunnel system that Olli usually escaped out of. "Take two, eh?" she wondered, pulling the cabinet open.

Razor chuckled and nodded a little. "How are you getting back to Big Town?"

Olli pursed her lips for a moment and shrugged. "I didn't really have a plan."

Razor's eyebrows knit together. "You didn't have a plan?"

Olli shook her head and half shrugged. "Not really."

"And you expected to just _walk_ the whole way?"

Olli shrugged. "I've got my jacket." She swung the black leather jacket around her shoulders. She shoved her arms into the sleeves and shrugged. "I'll be warm enough."

Razor stared at her for a moment and shook his head. "Absolutely not." He pointed to the chair. "Sit."

Olli looked at him and blinked. "What?"

"You're not _walking_ back to Big Town. You'll freeze before you get there."

Olli shook her head. "I'll figure something out."

Razor pointed to the chair. "Sit."

Olli walked back to the desk and face him. "I don't have to take orders from you, you know."

Razor caught up the desk phone that was at the far end of his desk. He brought it over and set it in front of her. He adjusted the long wire so it wouldn't get caught and gestured to it.

Olli looked at it for a moment and then looked back at him. "What's this?"

"It's a phone, Doll."

Olli clicked her tongue.

"Call Monte. Have him come meet you a couple blocks from here." Razor shrugged a little. "Stay in here where it's warm until he's close."

Olli looked at the phone. "Why?"

"Your father would have my hide if you caught your death out there. Your partner and Monte too." Razor chuckled and nodded to the phone. "Call, Monte."

Olli stared at the phone for a couple of seconds more before she sighed and picked up the receiver. She started to dial the number she <u>hoped</u> Monte would be on the other end of.

There were three rings.

"*Hello?*"

"Monte, it's me." Olli scoffed and half-shook her head. "You're never going to believe where I am..."

Olivia Wainwright, Big Town USA's District Detective, paused in the hallway and looked back the way she had come from before opening the small door between two studs in the wall. She didn't open it very far, just far enough to fit herself through the opening. Olli hesitated for a moment longer and glanced down the empty hall one more time, just to make sure that she hadn't been spotted, and pulled the door shut behind her.

Everything went completely black...

Can't wait for the next *Razor's Edge*?
Scan below!
Book 3 in the series due out Spring 2026!

Join The Big Town Mafia

WANT TO KNOW WHAT'S HAPPENING IN BIG TOWN
BEFORE EVERYONE ELSE?
JOIN THE BIG TOWN MAFIA
INCLUDED ARE:
MONTHLY UPDATES
COVER REVEALS BEFORE SOCIAL MEDIA
NEW COVER POLLS
BUY-IT-HERE-FIRST WITH NEW RELEASES
BEST OF ALL THERE'S AN ORIGINAL SHORT STORY THAT ONLY
THOSE ON THE EMAIL LIST GET TO READ!
JOIN THE BIG TOWN MAFIA
JUST SCAN THE CODE!

The One With The Review Reminder

Thanks so much for spending time with me in Big Town!
I really hope you enjoyed your stay.
Would you consider sharing your experience?
(Even just a couple of sentences!)
Your opinion will help new readers decide to buy!
Which means **more** people will visit Big Town!
Your words mean *so* much to me!
(And the new visitors of Big Town)
Just choose your favorite store (the more stores, the better!)
And let everyone know what you think!

The One With The Other Books

Unofficial Business Mini Series
Olli before she was The District Detective
Unofficial Business
The One With The Leather Jacket
***

The District Detective Series
Main Series
The Silence Broken
Baysnatch
Prussian Blue
Smuggler's Blues
Book 5 coming Fall 2025
Book 6 coming Fall 2026
***

Razor's Edge Series
A standalone series about what makes Razor, Razor.
Told by the man himself.
Fiddle Game
Pig In A Poke
Book 3 coming Spring 2026
***

The One with the Author Bio

J. Arens grew up on the Western Shore of Southern Michigan. Her days filled with horses, dogs, day dreams of fast cars and a love for great literary detectives. Nancy Drew, The Hardy Boys, Philip Marlowe, Sam Spade, Sherlock Holmes, and the brilliant but dangerous men who inhabit the pages of History during the time of the Volstead Act.

The District Detective series was born out of the need to read books that blended together the best things of all of J. Arens' favorites. All while set in Prohibition Era Middle-America.

When not working on the latest District Detective novel, or coming up with ideas for the next novel, J. Arens can be found attending local car shows, riding horses with friends, cuddling with police dog training drop-out, Dutch Shepherd mix, Dutchess and daydreaming about fast cars.